The Beauty -N- A Thug

The Beauty -N- A Thug
A Secret Love

QUANTABIA MANER

The Beauty_n_ A Thug

Copyright © 2019 by Quantabia Maner. All rights reserved.

No part of this publication may be reproduced, stored in a retrieval system or transmitted in any way by any means, electronic, mechanical, photocopy, recording or otherwise without the prior permission of the author except as provided by USA copyright law.

This novel is a work of fiction. Names, descriptions, entities, and incidents included in the story are products of the author's imagination. Any resemblance to actual persons, events, and entities is entirely coincidental.

The opinions expressed by the author are not necessarily those of URLink Print and Media.

1603 Capitol Ave., Suite 310 Cheyenne, Wyoming USA 82001
1-888-980-6523 | admin@urlinkpublishing.com

URLink Print and Media is committed to excellence in the publishing industry.

Book design copyright © 2019 by URLink Print and Media. All rights reserved.

Published in the United States of America
ISBN 978-1-64367-367-7 (Paperback)
ISBN 978-1-64367-366-0 (Digital)

24.04.19

PART I

THE EMERGENCE OF ZIAH

After 5 long exhausting years of undergraduate school majoring in biology, I was DONE. As I walked across the stage, I was more excited to be done with all the general information rather than feeling achieved. I felt no excitement at all for the degree itself just felt it was proof I've met my half way mark and the hard part is yet to come. I went into my thoughts for the remainder of the ceremony.

Leaving the undergraduate stress behind moving toward the goal at large.

College had kicked my but the first time around. It hadn't been at all like the experience portrayed on TV so often. I had my daughter and it was truly a battle within myself to get to the finish line. Right at this moment during my graduation ceremony I had drawn the conclusion of taking a year off from school. I was always told that it's a bad idea but I needed a break, I needed to relax, I need to be free. I hadn't had a chance to experience life and I needed some motivation to move toward the next level. I zoned back into the graduation ceremony and we were ready to toss our hats, but I kept mine because I was nowhere complete with my career goals.

After the ceremony I was greeted by my mom, aunt, daughter, grandmother, sister and best friend Calais. Calais and I have been best friends since middle school. We got off to a rocky start. We were two misunderstood individuals from different areas but same mentality. Once we took the time to get to know one another we have been friends down for one another ever since. Life has taken us through a series of radical events but our love never fades. My older sister and I have been best friends since I was born. We met in an unruly way as well but over the years have overcome ourselves to better know the other. She lives in Georgia working toward her law degree. She was always the type to want to escape from our small town feeling as if she was trapped with no hope. She avoided coming home or back, because she didn't feel it was home.

She claims she did a lot of studying but knowing my sister she knows how to relax. She taught me how to relax and not drown in my ability to focus so well. I didn't take her advice for undergrad school and I was feeling the affects of it.

I wanted to waste no time getting to the good part; the celebration. When it came to partying my family sure knew how to cut loose. Their obnoxious , unruly behavior was certainly about to pay the piper. Taylor, Calais and I all jumped into Calais's car and barreled down the highway to our destination. We arrived back at our family spot known as the cow porch. It was really just a patio that had been hand built by my uncle and a friend attached their house but it was ours. It was located in the woods behind the outskirts of the small town. It is well hidden and we are protected from civilization and law enforcement. The place was decorated and I could hear music and chatter behind all the cars once we pulled up. Calais had a leftover liquor bottle of Peach Exclusive in her car so we were taking shots. I entered into the cow porch and was swarmed with congratulations and hugs. I hugged and kissed my daughter and whispered, *thank you,* in her ear, acknowledging that behind it all she was and is my driving force to success. I entertained everyone who came to congratulate me but all I wanted was that sweet savory vodka that was in my peripheral. I was done with the focusing and it was now my time to let go. I wanted to embrace that girl inside me that never got a chance to rear her beautiful, unremarkable, comedic face. I was ready to laugh out loud and not care who it bothered. Just as I reached a cup, my Aunt Tina wanted to make a toast so I had to get a glass of champagne. She along with all the other women in my family were uniquely weird. She likes to make up rhyming names for everyone. She toasted and congratulated her Ziah Piah for a job well done. As the toast finished and everyone drank, I tossed my champagne back and picked up my Grey Goose vodka chased with sprite. My Aunt Tina laughed at me and pinched my cheeks. Hell at this point she could have done anything to me as long as I got my drink. As I headed to the back toward the pool Calais and Taylor walked in. I hadn't realized I had jumped out the car so fast and left them. I must have truly been thirsty or either they finished that bottle. I meant to escape out of the cow porch but became distracted, so now my Cousin Ann and Aunt Minnie wanted to take pictures. Great! We spent what seemed like hours taking pictures until it became the whole entourage diving into the pictures anyway they could. It would be the day I'm ready to party theses people are slow to get with it. They were on their own, I tossed my drink back and returned for the next. My mother was the bartender and knew I was ready to party. She was sure to give me double shots of vodka and was sure to let me know it was more where that came from. We walked to the back toward the pool as we exited the patio and into the smoking session my Aunt Gladys was hosting, *right on time,* was all I thought.

"Ziah, you and Calais smoking today?"

Calais and I looked at each other in agreement, laughed and took a seat with the others. My aunt announced since it's a special occasion we'd put three blunts in rotation. On my fourth hit, my sister pulled me out of the circle to bid me farewell.

"I'm about to go to the airport."

"What already we haven't had sister time?" I replied in a mellow tone.

"Yeah, I know but I have an exam tomorrow." Taylor informed me in a sad voice.

"Well, I guess have a safe trip home and do good on your exam." I said as I hugged her.

"Awe thank you little sister and try not to get too wasted. Then again.

Party, party, party. Be safe and stay away from the creeps tonight." She yelled while walking away.

I laughed at her comment because she has said that to me my whole life.

That seem like all she went for. She used to be a party girl. She stayed high and drunk. Then, one day she told me she talked to God and he led her to Georgia where she obtained a job. Which later turned into her seeking a law degree. We were raised in the church like many others but made the choice to experience life woes and all. However, no matter what we did or where we went the laws of our Lord remained in our hearts. We may have broken a few from time to time but then again who hasn't. We had some of the strangest conversations, arguments and altercations. Our minds had no limits and we both feel as though we are scholars so they are very interesting intense conversations that are really debates.

As the day went into night, our drinks had been refilled a few times and our minds distressed. We were having a blast. I had never really gone out and partied and was quite excited to venture out into this world. We were ready to take our moods out. I was ready to be free from any images, ready to be myself.

My mother appointed my little cousin Derek as our chauffeur for the night due to our drinking. He was the perfect man for the job being he was loud, obnoxious and bossy. He said what was on his mind and he made everyone laugh at his rudeness.

Everyone departed to get dressed and agreed we would all meet up at the spot. Calais and I giggled the whole time at nothing while getting dressed up until we reached the club. The parking lot was crowded and we were ready to get the rest of the night started. We strutted up to the door and we saw the others standing by the entrance giving off the same vibe we were feeling. Our atmosphere of serenity and fun lingered amongst us and it carried us into the rest of the night.

We walked into the club and immediately started vibing and bouncing to the music. At this point we were unbelievably drunk and didn't care who was looking we were in our zone having a great time. We all walked to the bar ordered two rounds of shots, tossed them back and made our way to the dance floor. It was about ten of us and we had not one care in this club. My cousin Sam pulled a blunt out of her purse and she handed it to me to light. She was the type to become boogie when she was wasted, She didn't want anyone in her space or around her unless invited. She became a troublemaker when intoxicated. Derek knew this so he made sure to move Sam to the middle of the group where she was surrounded by familiar faces. I just learned that at this very moment as I watched her make faces and slightly shove women and men from her personal space. I wanted no trouble just partying. I put fire to the loud musty scented object in my hand and took it straight to the head. Before passing it to her I inhaled hard, grabbed Calais, cupped my hands around her mouth and blew out the smoke. I choked her and she coughed for at least five minutes. I fell back in laughter and continued drinking. When the club ended Calais and I could barely stand so we used one another as a crutch.

Once the graduation night was over, we partied hard for the next few weeks but over the course of the weeks we had transitioned into a different type of partying. We had become friends with a group of guys we would have never thought to link up with. There were many and before we could relax we had to establish that we were here only to chill nothing more. Some had no problem with that, but some wanted nothing to do with us. We just wanted to chill, laugh, and drink with no worries or trouble, which is uncommon for girls in Passion City because they all had ulterior motives when it came to men regardless of their social standing. I honestly just wanted to party daily and these were the fellows to do it with. They partied everyday. We would come over early in the morning the time never mattered. It would begin with three to four of us and before dark it would turn into a full blown party session. I mean music, drinks, people coming by the masses and fun.

The summer weather was fast approaching and Calais and I was just beginning to let our hair down.

My daughter was spending time with my mother who decided to give me the time. I became consumed with the need to be free and unhindered. This was the first occurrence toward a new experience. I had begin leaving her with my mother or her father a lot often. I took on so much during school yet my main priority was my daughter. I tried to be superwoman and do it all but it weighed down on me in the end. The experience, I think, burdened me but I was ashamed to admit it. I felt like that was confessing I wasn't fit to be a mother.

I was going to need to truly relax to dive back into school. My mother is the one person who held my hand through school and having a child. I became pregnant with Avniel in my second year of college and trying to juggle being a good student and mother, it begin taking a toll on me. There were days when I had breakdowns and my mother flew to my rescue. She gave me words of wisdom, encouragement and motivation along with a bottle of Merlot. My mother knew that undergraduate school was only the beginning for me and my success so she made sure to stay involved in my life. She consistently pressured me to do things because of me being the youngest and most pampered I sometimes had to be pushed. We didn't come from money but my mother never allowed us to want for anything which is what led to Taylor and my mindset of whatever we want we can have.

We weren't raised by a strong, independent, determined, go getting, talented woman to have barriers in life. She taught us that the sky isn't our limit it's what we have to push through to get to the limitless. She raised us with a stern hand but a soft loving intolerant heart.

My senior year is when college life and home begin to really affect me as if something was trying to stop my blessings. I called on my sister so much during that year and she and my mother both would always tell me to take it to God.

This would frustrate me in the beginning. I then had no choice when there was no one to cry to or call on because of their own lives. I called on God in the name of His son and asked for strength, integrity and perseverance. I was brought up in the church, but as an adult is when I truly became familiar with God. Everyone looking at my life from the outside in, family included, felt my life was good and that I was getting all there was to be got, fiancé, child, security but that wasn't true. I talked to God everyday all day. I wanted answers on which way I was to be led in life. I wanted to fulfill the purpose I had been born for; I wanted my life to have meaning. I knew deep down inside that something in my life was missing and there was something I was being told to do. I didn't start feeling this way until my senior year in school. I had started to long for everything God had already aligned for me, the things he had laid out for me in his will. I desired to fulfill my true purpose in life to become a blessing unto God. I kept hearing a voice tell me to leave, leave my fiancé he was not the man for me but I felt that was just my insecurity because our wedding was getting close. I continued to have conversations with God and as my relationship with God grew my relationship with my fiancé begin to get rough. We started to argue more, fight and become filled with doubt and uncertainty. The voice told me, *leave Ziah, you must leave and take nothing except your daughter, leave it all behind.* I started to feel trapped and alone not able to confide in anyone about my thoughts except my sister. Due to her life experiences, her opinions about what I should do were uncertain because she adored my fiancé. I declared that I was ready to fall in love, to collide with the man that God had created for me. I wanted that true type of love that inevitable love, that can't be ignored, imitated or destroyed because it was in God's providential plan. As my relationship started to break down, that's when Calais begun to come in my life more. Things really took a turn when we missed our wedding date because through it all I was going to still marry him.

Fate had it so that it didn't happen and that's when I knew we were over. I just didn't know how to leave without hurting him or upsetting my daughter. This was the only life I knew and how was I to just turn so abruptly and walk away from it.

Then again what would I truly be walking away from?

Calais and I begin hanging out more because I had more time to spare. I found out she too was in a similar relationship hiccup but with a street dude which was a bit more physical but the same. We confided in one another and as we did our relationship grew stronger than ever before. My faith in God grew beyond measurability and even though I wasn't a diligent church attendee, I am a firm believer.

I listened to that little voice in my head more now understanding it was God directing my life's path. I still couldn't help but feel like I was missing something. I went searching for something with meaning, or so I thought.

Calais and I hung out a lot more and got in a bit of trouble from time to time. Our family and people close to us warned me about the guys in our choice of hang out areas. They were all receiving information from people about our new found friends. Taylor took it upon herself to lecture Calais and I about our 'friends' their ways and tendencies. Therefore, if I decided to interact with one, I knew what I was getting into. As time progressed, Taylor heard of me and another flocking to one another so she stayed calling me. I wasn't at all too sure of why I had started hanging out more, but in all honesty I felt like I wanted to do what I wanted do.

I had been sure to remain guarded while I had this time of hanging out, but this particular man of the street life had slowly and unnoticeably navigated his way to me, constantly, no matter how far I ran. The man who had caught my attention just so happen to be the biggest player in town and what society labeled him as, a thug. Taylor told me it was natural to be drawn in because that's what he wanted, but nothing honest would ever come from him because he belong to the streets. I have known many men of the streets, a few in my family, but never gone as far as to be involved or attracted to them, at least openly. My mom constantly warned me about the player types. She told me, *many women wanted to be the ones to change them but only ended up losing their hearts, trust, hope and futures. They are roughnecks that still your heart and break it.*

I steered clear of the street types since I was younger. Even then, in my tomboy stages, only one had the tenacity to grab my attention and fate just so happen that we'd meet up again but in a much more intimate way.

One Saturday in the middle of May, Calais and I were hanging in the yard with the fellas. We were all drinking listening to music and just vibing together.

Calais and I knew what hanging with these guys would get us, a reputation. I could care less. I had never met anyone remotely similar to our style or zone.

These guys act and functioned as we did except, they were street dudes as well as a few college boys and some older men in age. We all had so much in common, the chemistry amongst us all was undeniable and at this point we were invited into their lives as well as them into ours. Our party lives that is. We all got together randomly at times to drink, hangout and vibe. They all had girlfriends or baby mamas, so there was always drama on deck once word of us all kickin' it hit the air. These guys only kept girls around for one reason and it wasn't to share their feelings, yet Calais and I were always around or in the mist. Fox, Darkness and Slim were the three main guys we hung with, the others had jobs and lived out of the city. Our connection with these particular guys is unexplainable and I'm not sure how it even became a 'thing' but everything about it felt right regardless of their lives and reputations.

Our small town known as Passion City wasn't anything spectacular to brag about. It was a country small town in Southern Florida. One Sunny Saturday in Passion City, Calais, Me, Fox Old Man Smith and Darkness were all sitting around tossing back drinks while Fox was playing his old school music. We were all in a zone and throughout the day people came and went. The sun was something terrible shining as if it had a point to prove. I glared into the sun as an idea hit me.

"We should go half on a beach house for a few days."

Calais looked at me and smiled as if she had thought something similar.

"Hell yeah that would be fun. I say y'all pay for it though fuck half." Calais proposed.

"What? How the hell yall gonna suggest a trip on us?" Fox inquired as he tossed his bottle to the barrel. Darkness laughed as he rolled another blunt.

"What you mean we don't have jobs y'all do…sort of…yall making money."

Calais informed. Old Man Smith and I started laughing.

"We aren't fucking ya'll." Fox reminded Calais and I.

"So, damn you have to be fucking us for us to have fun, we may not be fucking y'all but ya'll can't get enough of us." Calais rebutted to Fox. I agreed as we slapped hands.

"Why don't y'all go shopping or something." Fox replied.

"Give us the money." I answered back. We all laughed because this was an all the time thing. Old Man Smith choked as he handed the blunt back to Darkness.

They never really had to come out their pockets, when we were around because we just like chilling and drinking. They're dope boys but we saw them as our bois and not as cash machines. Our relationship with them had gone deeper than anyone in Passion City would have or could have imagined. I saw them as friends and cared about them, I wasn't after what they had or could provide.

"You suck, you don't like to do shit with yo' old ass." I commented to Fox.

Darkness laughed.

"Hell naw, he ain't gone go." Darkness antagonized with me.

Fox and Darkness are years older than we are. We actually just "jumped off the porch" as they like to say.

Fox sat there with his middle finger in the air as we all three laughed at him.

"Fuck it, what the hell, let's do it." Fox caved.

Just as he declared he was in his girlfriend pulled up. We all begin teasing him about being on a leash because he had a hood rat that could care less about being a lady and prided herself on being hood and ghetto. She was the type of chick you'd give her a second, maybe even a third look, because she had the body of a video vixen and a fair face. However when she opened her mouth she had the voice of a chirping rat and the knowledge of a twelve year old.

I never understood why Fox was with this girl they just didn't fit one another. Then again Fox was with many girls, this is just the one he slept next to.

She had to deal with him and other girls all the time and we had made her list.

Fox, though a street dude, was very intellectual, charismatic, and caring. He had the reputation for being an inconsiderate, arrogant player. His exterior came off as cold and sheltered but only because he trusted no one, which Calais and I understood due to his career choice. His outside image was of a hard, heartless, dope boy and he grew accustomed to the demeanor but he wasn't at all what he portrayed. He just never had to be himself or get a chance to unless his guard was down. We heard so many stories about him and his crew as we were coming up in school so we kept our distance from him and Darkness. The fact that we embraced them was a bit odd and unexpected but they invited us to hang one random night, we accepted and we've all been connected ever since. Not the type of connected all the girls they've been with like to believe either, we actually knew these guys. They've seen us at our worst as well as we've seen them at their worst.

As his girlfriend walked up she begin scowling to see us all together, really just Calais and I. We all noticed her expression, so Fox stood and met her by the steps to usher her into the house.

Calais and I are school girls but since I've been hanging out in the hood, we've become known as fighters. No one knew of our bad attitudes besides our family, each other and now these guys. We were often told our appearances didn't match our attitudes. Calais is brown skin, 5'4", her hair was always long to her back no matter the style, thick thighs, a round butt, busty breast and extended eyelashes she loved to bat. She had a lot of tolerance and patience and you could never really tell she was upset unless you knew her. When she snapped, there was no calming her down she only saw red. Myself, 5'7" light skinned, shoulder length hair, full lips, thick thighs, busty breast and the face of the innocent. I looked sweet, and passive but I have a quick temper no patience and no tolerance. I sought after educating myself but come from a very aggressive and violent family. I hit first and ask questions later. We never really cared how the girlfriends felt, but I understood why they didn't like the setup. We are actually very gorgeous girls to be just chilling with, especially given the reputation of these guys so it made no sense. However, we all drank the same, never ending and like to party. Calais and I wake up drinking and continue throughout the day. Once we hit our limit, we regroup and go back in. The girlfriends often flipped out on them because of our presence, but Calais and I never got involved because we understood.

Fox came trotting down the stairs with three more beers as if nothing was wrong but we all knew sooner than later we'd be getting a show. He handed us our beer, Darkness was drinking Hennessy.

"So what's up, when we trying to leave?" Fox asked as he down his beer.

"Fuck it we all pack and meet up at my place to leave." Darkness proposed. Him and one of his baby mamas had a huge blowout a few weeks back so he made sure to keep his own residence just in case.

Calais and I agreed. "Don't be fucking bullshitting man." I exclaimed as Calais and I stood.

"You have such a dirty fucking mouth girl." Fox told me as he watched me while drinking his beer.

"Y'all have fun." Old Man Smith told us.

"I know." Was all I said as I winked at him and gave Old Man Smith a hug bye. He laugh out and proclaimed me as crazy.

"Have yall ass at my house in thirty minutes." Darkness demanded as he stood.

"Thirty minutes?" Calais questioned. "We females." She stated as she laughed.

"Ya'll don't need shit but bathing suits hell." Fox joined in as we walked to Calais's all black Infiniti coupe.

We threw up our hands as we entered the car. We left and went to eat because we already had our bags packed. We had planned on leaving already just thought to invite them.

We arrived to Darkness house an hour later because we decided to drink a bit at the restaurant. Both Fox's white Denali and Darkness's dark grey four door truck were in the driveway. As we knocked on the door we laughed knowing they would have something to say. Fox opened the door and we walked inside.

"Ya'll don't know how to tell time?" Fox interrogated us.

"Nope." I replied as Calais giggled at Fox.

"Hey bra, these muthafuckas fucked up!" Fox yelled back to Darkness.

Calais got off the couch and walked back to where Darkness was.

"This muthafucka still fucking packing!" Calais yelled up front to me.

I shook my head as Fox sat across from me staring. I laughed at him, but there was something different in his eyes. I'm a deep person and so is he so I was drawn in, his eyes were revealing. We both stared into each other and a feeling was exerted that I had never released before. Fox thinks he is so smart.

He think he going to knock me down on this trip. I refuse with all my might. I hope thats alot. I giggled at my thoughts and broke the stare down. He laughed at me laughing with no knowledge of my mind.

Fox and I sort of have history. Growing up, my older cousin ran with Fox and his street crew before he was murdered. My cousin and I, along with our siblings, were raised together so we all had a brother sister connection. I used to see Fox around but I noticed how he used to run through girls and make them feel as if they were nothing. Not just him, his entire crew. I think he was just the one on front street. He had no respect for anyone and let it be known. I told myself I would never be one of Fox's victims.

Between the whole crew they covered the whole town and then some. I did encounter two of the college boys, privately and found that even though they were much older than me it wasn't apparent during our 'encounters'. I was sure to stay away from the thug types growing up because my cousin would talk to me about the life and I would see him in his. He was so heartless at times but I knew his sensitive side so I was in love with his demeanor. Fox is what society considers a thug, ruthless, heartless, cold, dangerous, but he is the sweetest man underneath it all. When my cousin was murdered I shut down and became heartless myself, but then I had my little girl. I thank God because I know he gave her to me to prevent the life I would have led from my pain. It's taken me a while but I carry that same demeanor and understand it now. The exterior is what protects your heart and those who are held in it. I am not an inviting person and I check a person before ever allowing our paths to cross. When I am around those that I am not familiar or comfortable with I stay silent or separate myself. I trust no one and am not the type to be around unwanted company.

The look Fox was giving me was different. He wasn't just looking at me but into me. As he watched me I sat back on the couch and seen a different person. He's about 6' feet, light skinned, full lips, goatee, piercing brown eyes, dreads, and a mouth full of gold. This playboy was telling me something different in his eyes. He was lonely, desiring love, passion, trust, loyalty, something everlasting and I was in his sight. I smiled and as I did his eyes lit up and he smiled revealing his gold teeth. I knew I shouldn't trust what I was seeing because of all the things others said and proclaimed about him. What I had witnessed of him myself. Also I've been around him enough to know the way he thinks. He lacked respect for women. They were only good for one thing and it wasn't friendship. Then again I am being a hypocrite. I had been getting to know him for quite sometime and realized he can't help his sexual desires, he had issues. However, something was happening between us. We were saying nothing but revealing everything. I have always found myself with athletes or pretty boys and since I've been hanging out I've slummed a time or two. However as time passed I found myself more attracted to the thug types, guys from the streets. I was being introduced to them in a newer light. They showed me they have feelings. They just come underneath a lot of fucked up shit. He sat up and leaned down with his forearms on his knees, never breaking eye contact. I crossed my legs and bit down on my bottom lip while never breaking eye contact.

Our intimacy was broken by a knock at the door that turned into banging and ringing the doorbell.

Darkness came up front with a puzzled look and a pistol in hand with Calais trailing him. I took a look at Calais as she did the same and we made our way into the kitchen knowing it could only be one of their women. It was more along the lines of pulling Calais to the kitchen because she wanted to stay up front. Darkness answered the door to find it was Fox's and his woman. Calais and I couldn't help but giggle at the situation. We too had men but I'm unhappy contemplating walking away and she did as she pleased, so we didn't check in or call. They knew when Calais and I got together it was a done deal. They hated it but what could they do? Try to control us, but we'd eventually migrate back together. We have both been in relationships since high school, but we were being pulled toward something else and I had been drawn in. My daughter was safe so that's all that mattered to me. I sat on the counter and ate an apple while Calais poured her a cup of vodka. While looking for chaser she came across an already rolled blunt. We giggled. Darkness had forgotten a blunt from who knows when he probably suffered from memory loss he smoked so much. We took turns sniffing it before we lit it up to find it was hydro. The voices up front got louder so we knew they had entered the house. Calais and I crept out onto the patio, sat in the rocking chairs off to the side facing the doors, and smoked the whole blunt. As we got higher I started thinking *those girls already know we in here because of Calais's car.*

It took a while before they got the women to leave and it took a lot of yelling as well. Of course they brought up the third car in the yard but the guys never allowed them to make it to the patio. Calais and I laughed as we could hear them trying to get back to us but they never made it. We were stoned out of our minds when the patio door slid open. Fox and Darkness stepped out looking stress and irritated.

"So ya'll ready?" Calais asked nonchalantly.

"Ya'll high?" Fox asked. Calais and I laughed and went inside.

"You mufuckas ain't save me none, damn that's cold." Darkness complained.

"That was crazy. Wow! I'm surprised they left." I commented while finding my seat on the couch.

"Let's get the fuck out of here before those muthafuckas y'all call women come back." Calais suggested. She pulled her car in the backyard behind the high wooden fence.

We all loaded up into Fox's Denali and headed to the Key West. It was a six hour drive that Darkness did himself. He had rolled up blunts and he lit them the whole ride. It made me nervous so I didn't sleep, stayed awake and alert. I searched beach houses on my phone during the trip finding the best location.

It took no time to find the beach house once we were in the Key West. The boys dropped cash on it, so we were inside in a matter of minutes. The wooden house with huge glass windows facing the water had a porch connected with a Jacuzzi, three rooms, a huge kitchen, three bathrooms and living room. Calais and I wanted to share a room so the guys called us lesbians. From the get go when we arrived I noticed that we had paired off, guy girl. I don't think it was planned just sort of happened. I knew this was going to be an experience so I walked out onto the wooden patio to get some air and joined Darkness in his zone. He lit up a blunt and we zoned out while smoking it. Calais changed the spreads and sheets on our bed but I was ready to chill. When she walked out onto the patio the sun was setting and she had a cup. I giggled and shook my head as I got up in went inside to pull out my moscato. I put three ice cubes in the wine glass and poured the wine on top. I downed the first glass and refilled it.

I rummaged through the kitchen there was no food but the house came with dishes, furniture, power and a peaceful vibe. I walked out to join the rest but I only saw Fox; Calais and Darkness went to get groceries.

"Since we paid y'all cooking." Fox informed me of the terms and conditions. I laughed in my glass as I sipped it.

"That's a damn shame lazy ass, see that's why that white boy gone leave yo' ass." Fox proclaimed to me.

I laughed again. "Hope so, save me the trouble." I replied before I knew it.

"Oh yeah. What's going on?" Fox questioned.

I shook my head as to say I didn't want to talk about it. He said nothing more and leaned back while tossing up a Bud light. I tilted my head toward the sky with eyes closed to embrace the feeling of serenity. As I allowed myself to relax that feeling came over me which was enhanced by the wine and marijuana.

I slowly opened my eyes to see Fox staring out into the ocean lost in thought, I could feel his energy. The sun was setting which placed a reflection in the water.

"You happy Fox?" I asked him. He turned to look at me.

"Happy to be out here, not locked up, but not with my situation, you know what I mean." He replied honestly. I wasn't expecting him to answer me so truthfully.

"Yeah, so why you still there?"" I replied.

"You know, you get comfortable. You happy?" He asked me back.

"No but I'm about to get there." I truthfully replied.

"You been hurt before?" His question came to me as a shock. I paused before I answered.

"Not really, emotionally." I answered.

"You mean to tell me you let that cracka get to you." He blurted out.

"Shut up." He laughed and we continued vibing in each other's presence.

I wondered to myself how many girls got to see this side of Fox. He was comfortable and relaxed, his guard was down and that's when I realized mine was also. I've never been this unguarded not even for my fiancé and we have 7 years together. That feeling came again and my heart begin racing.

Calais and Darkness made it back with groceries but also some Popeye's chicken.

"What the fuck is this shit?" Fox questioned as the fast food was revealed.

Calais laughed hysterically as did Darkness.

"See y'all on that bullshit." Fox yelled.

"No it's late we all hungry now so we just got something, we gone cook muthafucka." Calais assured Fox through her laughter.

We all sat down at the island in the kitchen and munched out.

The night had approached and Calais had passed out after the food. I exited the room from showering to watch TV. Fox was sitting on the couch watching football so I sat down a space away on the couch next to him.

"Find something to watch." I demanded, he said nothing just flicked the channels.

He stopped at nothing so I grabbed the remote and put it on bad girls club.

"Ziah, I'm not watching this shit." He exclaimed while grabbing the remote.

He changed the channel and stopped on *American Gangsta*.

"No I don't want to watch this."

"We have to agree on something." He stated as he flicked the channels until he reached a movie called *Spliced*.

We agreed on the movie, he retrieved two beers from the kitchen and turned off the lights. He handed me one and adjusted himself in the corner of the couch. I grabbed a pillow propped it up and leaned back.

"You can lean on me move the pillow." He said as he moved the pillow. He open his legs and I scooted back toward his chest.

"Just don't be touching my dick." He warned me.

I laughed at him, "Shut up, you so dumb."

We chilled on the couch drinking and watching *Spliced*. I felt Fox rest his head on mine, and then he slowly and very softly caressed my arm. I'm drinking so his touch was intensified and my heart raced. I was unsure of where this unfamiliar feeling for Fox was coming from. Why had my perception of him changed? I was now at the conclusion that I needed to know if the chemistry was really that intense between us or if we were both just two sex freaks. I sat up between his legs and looked his way.

"What's wrong?" He asked concern while looking into my eyes.

I murmured to myself, "Let me see."

As I did I leaned into him and rubbed our lips together, licked his lips and kissed him. Just from the touch I knew this would be one of the most unforgettable kisses experienced. He kissed back with such passion, such desire.

He placed his hand on my back and I put mine on his neck. Our kiss was passionate; our tongues were having a conversation with one another, revealing every inch of our souls. I pulled away from him and sat back, I thought to myself, *oh shit*. He moved his left leg from around me and stood up over me.

"You done got off, now it's my turn." He stated while leaning down into me.

I tried moving from his path but he followed until our lips met again. He was on top of me as we were laid out onto the couch. He gently held my face with his right hand and made love to my mouth. I gripped each of his sides and his shirt indulged in the kiss. We were so deep into each other that we both begin to lightly moan. I was ready to give all of myself to him in that very moment. I had to pull away. I told him to get off me. He kissed my cheek and did just that. We both sat side by side in astonishment, from the feeling we now carried for one another, in disbelief of the feeling that had just been manifested. I don't know what he was feeling but I felt as he was my other half in that very instance from that kiss. I felt like I knew him, not just from being around him but in the past like we were intimate before. We never have been. All of these thoughts raced in my mind and I looked over to him and just as I did he looked at me. We leaned in for more kissing and I straddled him. He stroked my back and I wanted to know this man in every way possible. I kissed his eyes, his forehead then his lips. I had never felt like this for anyone before, this feeling was known, strong, unrealistic. I pulled back again and place myself on the floor in front of him resting on my knees. He looked wasted; his eyes were low, glossy and piercing.

"Why don't you respect women?" I asked him while sitting on the floor in front of him.

"I do, come here." He answered while reaching for me

"No you don't" I replied.

"I respect you." He blurted. I wasn't expecting that so I stared into him.

"I can't do this, you have a girlfriend and I won't do that to her." I informed him. I never mentioned my soon to be husband. He was left out of the equation.

He sat up and stroked his face, then stood up. "I respect that. I'm going to head to the room." I stood up and nodded.

"Can I have a hug?" I asked before we departed.

He walked up to me and we embraced, then I slowly directed him into the wall.

"I'm not gonna let you put me on the wall." He informed me.

His back hit the wall and I attacked his mouth. The passion was immediately in the kiss I could feel the heat between us. He rolled me so that I was on the wall next to the kitchen. I gripped his hair as he had a hand on my cheek and the other on my waist. I pulled away and led him to the counter. I sat on top of it and pulled him into my legs. He came willingly and we kissed once again. Our tongues exploring one another's mouth, my hands wrapped around his neck, his around my waist. I desired this man he had to be the man for me, our souls just meshed with one another. Our connection was like nothing I had ever felt. I placed my hand inside his pants but he stopped me. I looked at him and fell in love with him more; he stopped me from going further. I got off the counter and we departed.

I lied awake for hours in disbelief of what had just happen between Fox and I. What was that feeling? Was that normal? I had fallen in love with him just that quick but he was taken and I was in a situation as well. I thought to myself about all the warnings and words spoken about Fox. As I replayed the words from my sister, mother and the gossip always circulated about him, I had to think to myself if he was playing me. I had caught such deep feelings for this thug and he could be trying to lay me. I had become guarded at my thoughts and told myself to not fall for his charm.

The next morning the sun shined brightly throughout the whole place. I rolled over and went to the shower. I stood letting the water run down my body thinking about last night. I told myself that I would pretend as if nothing had happened. I would not become just another one of his conquest.

Darkness and Fox were in the living room watching sports center. Fox had a bud light and Darkness was smoking a blunt. I said nothing just started talking to Calais as she cooked.

"Well damn you don't see us. Good morning to you too." Fox yelled at me into the kitchen.

I didn't respond just looked up at Darkness and we both smiled. Just from that I knew I solidified my spot in his head whether he wanted me there or not.

Calais scrambled eggs, cooked sausage links and bacon, made toast as well as pancakes put out the orange juice and we headed to the patio. I could feel them staring us down as I walked onto the patio. Before completely exiting the house I yelled back, "Soups up."

"Soup, this breakfast time we don't want no damn soup." Fox proclaimed while he and Darkness walked to the kitchen.

He had become insistent on being a blatant jerk. I know him so that means he was trying to hide how he felt and his emotions by portraying that image the whole city has come to know him as. I grinned at his adolescence, but soon sadden at his inability to express love. What would this turn into if neither of us are willing to be vulnerable?

Minutes later Calais joined me on the patio in her red swimsuit and a mimosa in both her hands. I looked up at her and we both immediately laughed.

"What's up with you?" She questioned feeling something was on my mind.

I turned and stared into her for a while. She sat her cup on the small wooden table between us and waited for my response.

"Fox and I made out last night." I released as I took a swallow of my mimosa.

"What! How'd that happen?"

"I don't know we were on the couch chilling and things just took place...man he's an awesome kisser."

Calais took a gulp of her drink and then put it down to give the matter her full attention.

"Oh shit. Who made the first move?"

I smiled at her showing all my teeth. She burst with laughter and tilted her head back into her chair.

"Kill me now. Y'all both crazy as hell" She said while picking up her mimosa.

Before I could tell her the rest the guys came out onto the deck. I stared out into the water never making eye contact even though I could feel Fox wanting me to look at him.

"So, what are we doing today? Darkness questioned.

I stood, stretched and replied, "Don't know about yall but I'm about to jump on me a jet ski."

"Not me hell no." Calais yelled.

"Scary ass." I replied.

She laughed. "I don't give a damn, no…it's sharks out there girl."

I laughed at her comment and walked off toward the water. "Well let's walk the beach…y'all can do what y'all want."

"Ok." Calais agreed while still laughing.

"We don't need your damn permission to do shit." Fox informed me.

I turned around and glared at him about sick of the person he is giving me.

He stood glaring at me with a smirk on his face. I walk back toward him and snatched his hair.

"Girl don't be putting yo' hands on me… we gone have a problem."

I ignored him and rushed him. We became entangled in a wrestling brawl until we both hit the dirt.

"Ya'll trippin', I don't know what ya'll got goin' on." Darkness declared while walking pass us. "Come on, they on some other shit." Darkness informed Calais as she walked off eyeballing Fox having me pinned down.

"Get off me." I demanded from Fox.

He stood up and started dusting the sand off of himself and me. I'd never seen him willingly get dirty with his pretty boy ass.

"All this fucking sand!" I screamed while going up toward the house.

"You got on a bathing suit just go jump ya' ass in the water to rinse off."

Fox recommended while trailing behind me.

"Shut up."

"Girl, you rude as fuck." He stated while still trailing me up the steps.

"Why you following me?" I asked while turning around and shoving him in the chest forcing him down the stairs.

"I done told you about putting ya' hands on me Ziah, that's how you got dirty." Fox reminded me laughing and trotting back up the stairs.

I stood on the steps blocking him from getting up the stairs.

"Get yo' ass out the way Ziah. You want to do all this playing and shit."

Fox stated while trying to shove me out the way.

I wouldn't move so he walked up to the step I was standing on so we were face to face. I never noticed he had this softness in his face, his eyes gleamed and his lips were enticing. After standing in front of each other for a while without talking just taking in our passion and tension, I turned toward the sliding doors to the house. Just as I reached out to slide the door, Fox shoved me to the side and went inside. I reached forward once we entered into the door, I jerked his head back by snatching his dreads. As I did he spun me and shoved me into the nearest wall. I was pressed against the wall he held me by both wrists. We stared at one another saying nothing, our eyes said it all. The intensity of our eye communication sent my heart rate up which created an undeniable, unshakable tension in the room.

I bit down on my bottom lip and raised my left eyebrow unsure of what was going to happen but very interested. He released my wrist and backed away from our manifestation of feelings. I had energy to entertain his heart just didn't want to be bother with that other person. I reached forward and pulled him back into me by his shirt until we were body to body. Our eyes never left one another as I slowly stroked my hands up his arms across his shoulders and behind his neck. We both moved in to allow our lips to touch. I could tell he felt the same power in the kissing as I did because he was hesitant at first, giving pecks. I gave the back of his neck a stroke and his pecks turned into passionate kisses. I felt my body exhale, just as I did he gripped my right wrist pinned it on the wall, then slid his fingers in between mine and we both locked them tightly. I wanted this man as mine and only mine, I yearned for him. He removed my left breast out of my bathing suit planted soft kisses on it. My nipple entered his warm mouth and I felt my knees try to give out on me. I lifted the bottom of his shirt and stuck my hands into his shorts to be greeted by a hard, long thick guest. Realizing we were in a zone we created for just us two, I had to overcome this temptation and break away from this intense feeling, lust or passion, uncertain. Giving in right now would only give us both what we wanted now but not what we needed later. This man was used to getting any and everyone or thing he wanted. To make him truly mine, I had to resist and show him something better than what he was familiar with in his world. I shoved him off me and walked passed him back toward the sliding doors. He grabbed me and kissed me again. Oh how I wanted give him all of me but I couldn't. I snatched away again and walk to the beach.

I walked the shoreline deep in my thoughts unsure where this was going to leave our friendship. I begin regretting the actions, the love, all of it, because I didn't want to lose him as a friend. I walked in and out of the shops along the boardwalk until I could hold no more bags, and then went back to the beach house. I walked into the house to be greeted by Fox, Darkness and three unknown females. Looking at the scene I could feel my heart drop and the anguish building. Darkness dropped his head and made no eye contact but Fox sipped his beer and glared at me for my reaction. I wanted to flip out, but one thing Fox would soon need to learn about me is that I thrived on suppressing my emotions. I lived for it, because no one would ever know what my insides looked like. I smiled and spoke to the girls. I complimented their swimsuits. I made small conversation while not once looking at Fox then went into the room. I could feel the rage, the hurt, the pain, the feeling of betrayal all coming to the surface, I didn't like it. This man has no ties to me so why do I feel this way? He's just another arrogant hustler and means me no good. No one has ever had this effect on me or my emotions. Then again, I knew exactly who I was dealing with. I had known this was a possibility. I walked into this with my eyes wide open. I can't act like the victim in a matched situation. I could give two shits about anything but there was no running no hiding. It was here in my presence under the same roof so what was I to do? I had never experienced such disrespect and belittling.

However, I knew what and who I was dealing with, so now I would learn myself in the process of subduing the heart of my life long love. Even if it didn't end with us living happily ever after, I would always have his heart and occupy that brilliant brain. I had to shake this feeling before I acted irrational. It came to me like a lightning bolt, get even. I stopped pacing when the door opened, shutting the voices and laughter behind it.

"You alright?" Calais asked. I said nothing just nodded yes. "So what the fuck done happened?"

"I don't know girl. Nothing, which is the problem. I'm good though, but um…want to go out?" I asked while emptying out the bags I had.

She gave me a side look. "O' Lord."

I held up a multi-colored dress that came mid-thigh, thin strapped and the back out. The shoes brought out the gold in the dress. Calais is my best friend she knows things about me and my personality that no one does except my sister. She knew that this meant WAR. Everyone knows about my physical war tactics but Fox was about to learn about my mental war.

"That's mine? That shit hot girl!" She grabbed the dress and headed to the shower.

While she showered I laid across the bed feeling a fire burning my insides.

The stereo in the living room came on but I closed my eyes trying to find *the strength not to fuck some shit up*. I laughed out loud at my thoughts and asked for forgiveness, and just like that my spirits were lifted. The fun was on the way. I was going to make him regret ever mistaken me for one of the girls from back home.

I pulled out my all black sleek silk dress, the neck line dipped down pass the breast, a red fitted belt wrapped around it under the breast into a "V" and the back dipped the same. I pulled the red boot stilettos out of the other bag and stood in the mirror deciding how I wanted my hair. My moods slowly begin changing. I turned on the room radio. I popped open a beer from our fridge and lit a blunt courtesy of Darkness. I smoked until Calais walked out of the bathroom. I stood, handed her the blunt and went into the shower. I heard her yelling, *o' shit,* o*' shit*, and then she laughed. The blunt and beer kicked in and I felt sexy showering. I washed every inch of my body with care and sincerity, I was high. I walked out of the bathroom to find Calais still puffing on the blunt. I reached for it and swayed to the music as I smoked the rest. I noticed she had been drinking my beer so I laughed at her. She joined in and I could tell our night was going to be magnificent.

We were dressed, ready to leave an hour and a half later after getting ready and smoking another blunt. Calais and I were both high and feeling good.

We posed for our camera phones and headed out the room door. When we stepped out everyone paused. The girls praised our dresses and how beautiful we were. Fox stood up and Darkness dropped his head again.

"Where the fuck ya'll going?" Fox questioned, I looked at him and smiled.

"Out." Calais answered for me.

"We suppose to be a group ya'll ain't invite us."

"And y'all didn't invite us to y'all gathering!" Calais screamed as we walked out the door.

We caught a cab to uptown where all the clubs were and chose one. We walked into a club called Tipsy. We paid for a table in the back courtesy of the fellas, of course they didn't know.

It was crowded, wall to wall and the scene was a mix between hip hop and R&B. We had a bottle of Grey Goose vodka brought to the table along with some chaser. Our first drink, we had shots, we were ready to get the party started. We both stood and worked our section having bottles sent to us from other tables. We lost count of our cups and our bottles the night was ours to take. Just as we felt the night couldn't get any better we looked up to see some familiar faces coming toward us. Fox and Darkness had found us. Calais and I laughed hard at the sight but I truly was relieved and felt like round one went to me. Now I'm not the type to play games when it comes to the matters of the heart, however in order to own what's going to be mine, I had to enter his world. Draw him into mine, then create our own. I could see in his eyes he wanted me just as much as I want him but he didn't know how to get me. I was out of his element and to be even remotely close to me he had to step out of his element as did I.

"All these damn bottles, I know y'all ain't pay for' em." Fox stated immediately as he walked up to our table.

Calais and I said nothing just laughed. Darkness fired up a blunt, smoked it and passed it to me. I smiled as did he knowing Fox had met his match.

"Drink up muthafuckas!" I invited.

We had several vodkas, Hen, and buckets of beer from our surrounding male neighbors.

We picked up where we left off dancing to the music enjoying our night. I turned to pass Darkness back the blunt from Calais and found Fox piercing me with his eyes. I smirked knowing I was getting to him just as much as he was getting to me. I could see he wasn't prepared for me. He had underestimated who I am. I turned around and danced more feeling great, then I thought about my thoughts and laughed out.

The club was ending so we all walked down from our table to the exit. On the way out a dark skin tall broad guy with a mouth full of gold grabbed my arm and pulled me to the side. It couldn't have been more perfect if I had set it up.

Fox tried not to stare or even look but he wasn't as strong as I when it came to hiding emotions. I wasn't interested in the guy just took his number to piss off Fox.

The whole way home no one said anything Calais and I just giggled. We arrived to the house and I decided to get in the Jacuzzi with a glass of Moscato to relax. Everyone else had retreated to bed but I wanted to see the stars, feel the moon and hear the ocean while relaxing in the hot Jacuzzi. I tilted my head to soak in the air and release all the stress that was lingering over me. I became deep in thought about Fox and my situation.

How is it that we are here acting as two love sick strung out puppies over one another and we have people back home. I think I may feel more deeply about Fox then my boyfriend. I wonder what Fox would do if he found out I was suppose to be getting married? What the hell am I going to do with a damn thug anyways. Why the hell are we even up here with them? This was bad from the jump. I can't keep pretending as if I'm not aware of who I've been hanging with. I am pretty awesome. I'm intelligent, funny, laid back, down to earth, easy on eyes, I knew it would be a stretch trying to be friends. Who am I trying to kid? Everyone. Two guys and two girls, this was crazy to do, I wonder if Calais and Darkness have done anything?

I laughed at all my random thoughts to find I wasn't alone. Fox came out and sat in the chair behind the Jacuzzi. I moved to the other side to get a view of what was going on.

"So what'd you do with that number?" Fox interrogated wasting no time.

I smiled at his question. "What'd you do with those chicks?"

He chuckled and dropped his head, "So you a vengeful mu'fucka, eye for an eye type of shit." He stared at me as I smiled, then winked at him.

"You betta stop that shit." Fox warned. I smiled again.

"You coming in?" I invited.

He didn't answer, just watched me so I tilted my head to the sky. I looked over at him as he took off his shirt to reveal his hairy chest with his toned muscles underneath. I laughed thinking to myself he should have a gut given all the beer he drinks. He slid down into the hot tub on the opposite side of me. He grabbed a remote out the pockets of his shorts on the ground and I noticed speakers on the wall. I smiled as the R&B came streaming through the speakers.

I looked at him as he did the same. I could feel the magnetism between us and knew we were both in trouble at this point. This was no weekend splurge and I'm not sure how long these feelings have been being suppressed by us both. These emotions run too deep to be manifested over night, but we did have a friendship as well. I finished my first glass of Moscato and poured another.

"You better slow down." Fox suggested. I smiled at him and drank some more.

"You gone get drunk and I'm a take advantage of you." He tilted his head back toward the sky.

I chuckled, "You can't I drink just as much as you."

He said nothing just made an agreeing noise under his breath.

I wondered what kind of life he had? What was his thoughts?

How the hell did we come to intertwine to this magnitude? I went to college just to fall in love with a thug from home. The irony was uncanny, full of weird associations that led us to be at this point. I know what I was told about Fox. I believe I just wanted a chance to love my broken down, untamed, rude, hurt, battered and afraid soulmate. Our chemistry drew me in every time we were alone. We know everything about each other, flaws and all, I still wanted more. I was pursuing him but allowing him to feel like he was calling the shot. I had many years to learn how to maneuver around men just to get to this one.

I stood revealing my blue two piece bathing suit and made my way toward him. His eyes opened and he begin laughing at the situation. He threw his hand up trying to stop me from infiltrating his area but he didn't put up much of a fight. He was growing intimidated by my womanhood that he had no idea I possessed. I straddled him in the water, caressed his thick eyebrows, rubbed my fingers in his dreads, then wrapped my arms around his neck.

"You a fucking tease. Why you keep fucking with me?" Fox asked refraining from touching me.

"What'd you do with those girls?" I asked ignoring his remarks.

He looked me in my eyes and told me, "Nothing," while shaking his head.

"Promise?"

He nodded his head in agreement.

"Say it."

He rolled his eyes, "Promise."

As soon as he said it I embraced his mouth with mine. His hands moved from the deck to wrap around my waist tightly as if he never wanted to let go. I had a hard time believing him, but I loved him.

We made it back to Passion City that following Tuesday and everyone went there way with no comments just memories of our special vacation.

I went and seen my daughter as soon as we got back in town took her out and spent time with her. She was the only thing stopping me from walking away.

I didn't want to upset her in anyway. She adored her father. I know if I were to leave he wouldn't be the man he portrayed while we're an item. While visiting my daughter my mom had a lot she wanted to talk about with me.

"Hey Ziah."

"Hey Ma'. " I greeted back.

I sat down on the sofa and begin flickering through the channels.

"Ziah.." My mom called as she dusted her house.

"Yes." I responded while finding something to watch.

"You hanging out with Fox?" She asked.

I sat in silence saying nothing.

Her question sent a wave of shock through my body. Hearing his name sent my heart in a panic that I felt she could see.

"What, why would you ask me that?" I interrogated trying to keep my own panic down.

"I was just wondering. Y'all having sex?"

"What ma'? Where are you getting this?"

"Well you know I'm gone ask Ziah."

Wednesday came and I found myself lounging out on my apartment balcony deep in thought hiding from my fiance. He and I hadn't even kissed since I've been back from the vacation. My mother's interrogation sent me in a world wind of thoughts about my relationship.

I don't know what to do. Should I leave? Should I marry him for my daughter's sake? I would be miserable because truth be told I couldn't stop thinking about Fox, what he was doing, who he's with, if he's being smart, safe, okay. What would I do with a thug, their lifestyle is too hectic, and I've got a kid. Would Avniel even like Fox? Would he like her? Why was I thinking about them liking each other? The kissing fling would be a one time thing, ugh...what is wrong with me? Fox is just a player trying to get wherever he can. Ziah you must not lose sight of that.

My thoughts were interrupted by the chiming of my phone. Cal popped up on my screen.

"Yeah? What's up?" I answered.

"What you doing?" Calais asked on the other end of the receiver.

"Smoking on the balcony." I responded. We both laughed.

"Shameful. Fox said come drink." She blurted out.

I said nothing just paused.

"Hello?" Calais called out.

"Where at? His house?" I responded.

"Yeah. The yard."

I paused again.

"You coming tramp?" Calais inquired.

"Yeah."

"Alright."

I hung up the phone and smoked another blunt. When we arrived back in town I put my engagement ring on. I forgot to remove it going to Fox's. I wore it while I got stoned to see how I felt about the idea of being married. My thoughts were much more intense and efficient while I was stoned, at least I thought so. I stepped out the car to find Calais, Old Man Smith and Fox sitting on the picnic table with cups. The music was streaming through the speakers and Calais and Fox looked buzzed. I walked up slowly. Fox lifted his head when he saw it was me his eyes sparkled and his face lit up.

How could I not be in love with this gorgeous intelligent thug? His exterior is so rough and his face tells a story, but he still had a soft heart. I wanted to save him from himself. Show him what life had to offer that he wasn't and didn't have to be a victim to his circumstance. I wanted to marry him. I knew this was only my thoughts and I must refrain from my emotion around him. He is out to hurt me. So why keep going? I know it's fucked up but I wanted him to want me to a point that he could never get over me. I sought to make sure if I walk away with a broken heart, so would he. I guess I sought to do to him as he did to all the women before me. I wanted to break him so I could love him. Damn, it's a good thing we didn't have sex because I am just as fucked up with issues as he. I looked the part but if they only knew my mind.

"Hey folks." I spoke in a mellow tone.

Fox burst with laughter and dropped his head.

"You high." Calais proclaim through her laughter. I said nothing just gave her a smile showing all my teeth.

"What's that on your hand?" Fox asked while looking at my hand.

Calais looked at me and rolled her eyes. She knew what I had been doing.

"OH, that's my engagement ring." I responded while looking at my hand.

Fuck how did I manage to forget to remove the thing. It's so beautiful though.

"Oh you engaged? Since when? Since we came back?" Fox interrogated.

Calais held her head down only picking it up to sip out of her cup.

Old Man Smith walked over to get a better look at it.

"For about a year." I responded truthfully.

"Nice." Old Man Smith remarked.

"A year, this the first time I'm seeing the muthafucka and we've been hanging for a minute now." Fox replied.

I didn't respond not in the mind state to have an argument with him.

"How many carats is it?" He inquired.

I looked down at it, "2.85 morganite, pink my favorite color."

"Well if he really loved you it would be 5." Fox informed me while walking into his house.

When the door shut, Calais and I looked at one another in shock then we laughed. Darkness and Slim pulled up as the thunder started rolling in. We all retreated into the house, no TV only music just talking and vibing with one another. The conversation shifted to marriage somehow. I asked the men if they believed in marriage, true religious vows in front of God marriage. Slim revealed he had been engaged but it was a disaster and he would never trudge that hill again or far in the future. Darkness said he believed in marriage to the right woman, which threw me since he and his chick have been together for over seven years and they have two kids. Fox was the one who had to be an asshole about it.

"Ziah you know black people don't get married they just be together for a long ass time."

"I believe in marriage, you be with me you gone have to marry me. I want papers on your ass." I replied firmly. Everyone laughed at my comment.

"Come on now we have to compromise because you know black people don't get married." Fox confirmed.

"I do, I want to get married." I repeated while glaring at him. He dropped his head, laughed then sat back and drank his beer.

Several months passed and things changed on my home front. I moved back in with my mom hoping to soon get a job and get out on my own. Calais and I ventured out and found a small hood spot in the county over. We had started going there to get away from our lives and the city. Things had gotten weird.

Every time we went out Fox would have broads all around him. I guess there was nothing different about that just the way I was feeling toward him. I never did tell him that I was no longer engaged or in a relationship. The last time we went out in the city Fox's chick had made a scene at one of his parties as did Darkness's.

They had started getting out of control so we backed away to avoid any unnecessary drama.

Friday night rolled around in the middle of October and Calais and I decided to show our face out. We went out already tipsy and had a blast. We posted up in our corner, laughed and moved to the music. After the club I ran into a guy who intrigued me. He was a sophomore in college and on the football team as a lineman. I've never been attracted to a big guy before but there was something about him that caught my attention. He carried himself as a mature man, with a dope boy's charm. We stood and talked outside of my car and as we were exchanging numbers, the car parked beside us moved and I looked up to see Fox surrounded by a group of girls. He frowned when he saw me and the guy exchanging numbers. I got in my car and Calais and I left.

The following Monday we ended up at Fox's house chilling with more than just the usual. Since our absence, more people started to hang out at Fox's. Fox said nothing to me, and the heat had us all playing musical chairs trying to escape it. Fate had it that when we all got comfortable, Fox and I were side by side. I turned to see him on my left and Darkness on my right. When I looked at Fox he said nothing just glanced at me and dropped his head. I knew there was something bothering him but there are too many people to address it.

Darkness was curious about Calais and I as women. "How many dudes have y'all been with?"

I laughed at his question.

"Wow!" was the only thing Calais could get out.

"I've been to college is all I'm going to say." I stated.

One of the other guys responded.

"What does that mean?"

"What I said, I've been to college, take it how you'd like." I repeated while laughing.

"How many girls y'all think we've been with? Between us three?" Darkness inquired about him, Fox and Slim.

I laughed, "The whole damn city."

"And then some." Calais added.

"Damn." Darkness replied while laughing.

I got up and went inside to retrieve more beers. A few seconds after me,

Fox walked in behind me. I turned to see who it was and seen him locking the door so I stood up from the fridge. He started walking toward me.

"When was you gone tell me you left the white boy?" Fox asked without flinching.

"When was you gone tell me you dropped ya' scalawag?" I replied back.

He said nothing and neither did I. Obviously we had been keeping up with one another even though we haven't been around.

I wonder what else he knew about in my life. Where was he getting his information, not Calais cause she would tell me and he had too much pride. It had to be someone he really trusted and confided in…

"You need to stop going missing all the time." Fox told me.

I smiled at his comment because I saw his heart. "Why you been missing me?" He said nothing in reply just looked away. "Awe, you do that's so cute." I responded to his silence.

I sat down the beers, reached out and grabbed the lower part of his all white tee. I reeled him into me until he knocked my hand down.

"Naw Ziah, you not fixing to be playing these games with me."

I smiled and tilted my head to the side. "Don't be like that Fox." I replied.

I grabbed his shirt again and reeled him all the way to my body pushing me back on the fridge.

"You gone stop playing with me."

I slid my hands to the back of his neck and locked my fingers together. His hands gripped the side of my waist firmly like he needed to be held up, as if touching me made him weak. I kissed the right side of his neck, his Adam's apple, his left side then I caressed his dreads. He moved his hand up to my neck and pinned me lightly on the fridge. He had never done this but I was turned on by it. I could sense he was battling between a love-hate feeling. I caressed his cheek with my right hand and caressed his chest underneath his shirt with the left. He closed his eyes and leaned his forehead on mine. Something was wrong; something was going on with him and it bothered me not to know. I gripped his face with both hands to bring his eyes to meet mine.

"What's wrong Fox?" I softly whispered.

Just then someone started beating on the door. Fox turned to go answer it but before he opened it he looked at me and said, "You need to stop disappearing."

I grabbed the beers, turned and as I did the door swung open. It was a light skinned female I had never seen before. He let her in and hugged her as I walked passed to head back to the picnic table. Once again I held my emotion through my pride, not to let anyone see me give a reaction. I handed out the beer and took a seat.

Now once again he's with this hard man mentality. He's afraid of his emotions, he don't want a woman, but a skeeze he has to put little effort into. He's afraid of me and what I make him feel, he being a big dawg…big fucking whore is what he is! I giggled to myself at my own thoughts.

Weeks had gone by and I hadn't seen the boys at all. I found myself home more thinking of ways to get to school. Or find a well-paying job. When the pressure and thoughts filled my brain I called up Calais to party. I love her dearly because even though we both caught grief from our men when we need one another, we will drop it all to console us. Calais and I weren't the type of females to be openly emotional. We never let outsiders know how we are feeling.

Through all our pain and hurt we hold a solid face, but in the comfort of each other we are emotional females trying to figure out this thing we call love.

I can say not many know how deep my love, passion or desire for Fox is.

They all think it's me wanting attention and power. In the minds of those in Passion City I had become just another one of Fox's conquests that wouldn't let go. I disputed nothing and I showed no difference. I allowed my city to continue to falsely exalt him as the coolest, smoothest, unbothered playboy of all time. I allowed that of them for him because I sought nothing other than his heart and when I finished, it would be revealed, flaws and all. They had no clue what I had done to their sweet, untamed, rude, party loving woman slayer and it would remain our secret.

Lying here on my bed while my daughter laid on me watching cartoons, I reminisced about one of the night's Fox and I spent.

I called him to check on him due to him getting ridiculously plastered the day before. As I did he invited me over so I went. We sat on separate couches in his house watching 'Martin'. Given our last encounter during our beach house vacation, he wanted us to keep a distance because he felt I was a tease. We argued about all the girls. Well I argued about the girls and how I felt he should cut them off. I told him he should cut them completely a loose because they didn't want him but what he had or what he could do for them. He argued at me about not giving in to the sexual urges we had for one another. He insulted me saying he could find plenty of girls like me. As he said it, I was hurt and offended.

I sat back on the couch and watched the television. We both sat in silence and all I kept hearing was his damn phone vibrating. Of course we both were drinking so I reached over and snatched his phone out of his hand. He came over to my couch to retrieve the phone but we ended up in a passion filled lovers quarrel. He kissed my neck rubbed up my body and I leaned up to meet his lips. He quickly snatched away but we stared into each other. That light touch sent a rush of passion throughout our bodies that was indescribable. He kissed down my chest to my breast and placed them in his mouth. As he nibbled my nipple he grabbed my hand and intertwined our fingers together. No matter how bad I wanted to give in my mind said no make him wait. My body screamed for him to come inside. Me being a college girl I followed my mind knowing in the long run it will benefit me in the pursuit of what I wanted out of him.

Fox has stopped trying to have sex with me. I haven't seen him in weeks but this weekend I wanted to go out and forget about my worries. Calais and I had finally begun to slow down on the partying. We both agreed we needed to get focused. I stayed consumed with thoughts of making my own way in life with my daughter by my side. I begin to get down on myself because I couldn't find a job. I wanted a career not some penny paying job that I could barely survive off of. I wanted so much out of life along with my career, and now I also wanted Fox.

I often thought of us being married, making a home keeping one another well satisfied and happy. I felt like an idiot, I know this man couldn't be mine because of the life he lives and has grown accustomed to. My dreams were much bigger than Passion City or the state of Florida and no one or nothing would deter me from my goals. Then again I felt like the smartest female he'd encountered because I had his heart, mind and soul by doing nothing but allowing him to get to know me. Through all the arguing and frustration, I am still so deeply in love with him and the thoughts filling my head are of the good times and I'm not sure if that's saying the good outways the bad or me being naive. I really can't stand how I feel about Fox and I don't know if he feels anything for me. My feelings are so strong they are hard to contain at times but I know regardless of what happens between us, this is a part of life and if I must, I have to overcome this to move forward.

Calais was trapped inside with her boyfriend and she was the only one I feel comfortable with hanging with. I wanted to get out the house, I wanted to occupy myself and relieve my mind of all the thoughts about my desired life. I lay across my bed not wanting to call anyone to accompany me out, so I decided to step out by myself. I rode out to the club, in the woods of our small town. It is our hole in the wall. I laid low in my car behind my mirror tints drinking my vodka straight no chaser. I was on a mission and that was to party. I watched everyone without anyone knowing I was inside the car. Once I started to feel lighthearted and cheerful I knew my alcohol had begun to work. Before stepping out of my car I prayed to have a good time and protection from all hurt, harm or danger.

How many would find this to be a contradiction in itself and the conservative Christians would frown upon this action. I feel as though we are told and taught to take God with us everywhere and every single last one of us are sinners regardless of our church standing. So why shouldn't that apply when we are out in the world? Wouldn't one agree this is the time we should call on him the most, look to him with faith? I could never talk to someone of great Christian standing and faith about this because they would say the purpose of taking him everywhere is to walk with him, give your life to him. My thoughts are, how they would know whether or not that person hasn't already given their life to God?

They could still be learning and fighting the battle within themselves for the time being. No, conservative Christians believe the only way to God is through the church but in reality it is through His son Jesus Christ.

We are led by flesh and must call on him as much as needed to fight off ourselves.

I giggled at my sermon I had just given to myself and exited my car. I wore my all white heel boots, my ripped faded dark blue jeans and an all-white ladies tank. I loved to dress casual yet classy it always worked in any atmosphere. I was definitely feeling myself I could feel it in my walk. I walked toward the entrance and was greeted and complimented by a few 'old friends'. I laughed to myself once again as I entered into the building to think:

All the blame I put on Fox about his women habits but I too have my secrets as well. I have a few close to him as do he to me. I get so discourage to think about the women he invite into his bed but I must consider how he feels to know we have something special yet I invite others into my bed. His indiscretions are put on front street because he does his in the open, me, I'm more of a private person and move better in the dark. Right to this day no one even knows about Fox and I relationship, the connection we share. They can only speculate because I am not the type to want everyone knowing what I am doing. I don't want him for recognition or a prize. I want him because regardless of what others see I know him and he deserves a decent chance at life. He deserves to feel the love that I carry for him because in my mind, I am made for him and he is the only man I believe that can keep up with me.

Consumed in my thoughts I was approached by one of my secret friends at the bar. I called him, *Tar*, because he was just that dark. He and I made an unexpected friendship that was mistook and led to us having sex. I didn't want it to go that way but due to our bond he took it there forcefully and I gave in and turned it into what he made it. He was already in a rocky relationship but once we started kicking it, he believed he had fallen in love with me. That's how most of my relationships went but it never lasted more than 3 months because I always felt my heart was with someone else, which it was…in Fox's pocket. I smiled while biting down on my bottom lip to feel him pressed against me staring. I turned to be met by his insanely sexual glare. We both stared at one another reminiscing about the sex we use to have because regardless of the place or time it was really good. I dropped my head feeling my liquor take over because I could feel my eyes giving off a sex signal, this tended to happen when alcohol was involved.

I must remember not to lead him on because he is the aggressive persistent type that didn't take no for an answer. I liked controllable aggression, but I didn't like all the stalking and forcefulness to be something more.

"Where your sexy red ass been?" He asked in a low whisper in my ear. I laughed at his question.

"Around." I replied through my smile.

"You gone call me later?" He asked while discretely placing his hand on my lower abdomen.

I paused and looked at him with my eyebrow raised at the placement of his hand. Then I knocked it down and just as he was moving in closer, I was bumped which pushed him back. I turned to be greeted by a pair of eyes that would have stabbed me over a thousand times if they were knives. Fox said nothing just stood at the bar and ordered a bottle for his table. I dropped my head and faced forward while *Tar* walked away from the bar. I waited next to my destiny for my drink and had nothing to say. I could feel him staring at me but I wouldn't make eye contact. My drink was up, I grabbed it and walked away from the bar with no hesitation. I made my way to my corner by the speaker and exhaled.

The place was dark and I could feel the others watching my every move given that I was out alone. I watched Fox walk back to his table with the bottle and noticed the girls who looked thirsty for his attention. Once again I dropped my head and sipped my vodka not wanting to upset myself with unnecessary thoughts. I shook off the feeling that wanted to creep up on me and tuned out my thoughts to tune in the music. My body sway and my muscles started to relax. As the night progressed I couldn't stop laughing to myself at the situation I had come across after all the years of avoiding them, thugs. Several guys made their way in my space wanting to approach me but not knowing how so they lingered and offered me drinks. I felt beautiful but that was because I pictured how I looked in my head and it turned me on. As I enjoyed myself it showed in my body language and it was like I was giving off a signal because more men surrounded me. I had zoned out, but when I realized I was being surrounded it made me uncomfortable. I had gotten distressed. I got what I came for so I felt it was time to go. I slowly and with charisma, strutted to the door to be sure not to hit the ground as I have before and headed down the field to my car. I smiled the whole way there and *thanked the Lord for protecting me.*

I sat in my car and laughed hysterically to myself because all the time I spend thinking of Fox, talking to Calais about Fox, when I see Fox I play as though he's just another man. I started my car up, and then there was a knock at my window. *Man I hope it isn't Tar.* I opened my door to be greeted by Fox. He said nothing so I stood up out of the car.

"Heyy." I greeted him not knowing what else to say.

"What's up? So you weren't gone say shit to me?" He asked aggressively.

"What am I supposed to say to you Fox?"

"Oh, so it's like that now?" Fox asked putting some space between us.

"Fox, you are doing what you do best, being Fox. Well, I don't know what to say to Fox that every chick you encounter hasn't already told you, however to Travis, it must suck to be surrounded by so many people and yet still feel alone."

"I don't want to play games with you Ziah." Fox revealed to me and I could see his vulnerability, his heart.

"Well don't, but then again that's asking too much from Fox, right." I stated as I sat back in my car with the door open.

"Ziah what you want from me?" He questioned with anger.

I stood up and pulled him into me by the lower part of his bright red shirt.

"Travis I want nothing from you… all I want is this…" I stated while pointing at his head.

I wanted his mind, his heart, his soul, all the rest would be nothing without him.

He stepped back again creating space astonished by my answer. In sync we realized we were outside of the club having this conversation so we both looked around. There was only one person to witness our discussion which was Darkness's brother Les. Fox and I said nothing, I got in my car and he walked back toward the club.

I drove away not looking back in my rear view mirror but I felt my chest heave, my breath pick up, and my eyes swell.

Don't do it Ziah, don't you do it. Just pull it together. Let it go. It's okay, you're a beautiful woman, let him go. There will be better, it's just not meant to be. Don't waste your talent, love and warmth on a man that doesn't want it. O' God please help me right now, give me the strength to press on and overcome all obstacles. Lord our Father not my will but yours be done. Lord I am in pain, my heart hurts for this man and even though I know you don't work in the matters of falling in love, I ask that you heal my heart Lord. Remove this man from my life completely if it's not true. If what I feel is not true and full of lust please Lord give me the strength to move on and take him and his falsehood from my life. I feel for this man in my soul, so very deep and don't want to be a victim to worldly things.

Avniel is with her father so I kept driving. I realize I have spent little time with her, but I was going through a period of discovering myself, my life, me. I didn't know where to go, but I had to get out of this town for one night. I had to escape just for a moment to clear my thoughts. I drove unconsciously lost in my thoughts until I arrived at the beach. I parked and heard the waves crashing down from the parking lot. I grabbed a folded blanket out of my trunk and a forgotten bottle of pink Moscato. I walked down toward the shore. I found a spot not too far from a couple lost in each other's mouth. *Great!* I thought to myself but spread the blanket out and enjoyed the breeze and the silence, nothing but the waves crashing to the shore. Lying in the sand my silence was broken by the chiming of my phone. I forgot that was in my bosom. I didn't recognize the number so I pushed end. A few seconds later the number popped up on my screen again, I pressed end. Immediately after it chimed again, *goodness I hope it's not Tar, he's so freaking aggravating, a bit weird and scary as well.*

"Hello…" I answered faintly.

"Where you at?" The familiar voice asked with authority.

"The beach. What's up?" I asked nonchalantly.
"THE BEACH!!? What's up there?"
"The water, silence, me and a bottle of Moscato."
"A'ight." Fox responded. "I'll let you enjoy it then."
I said nothing in response just hung up.

I wondered where he got my number from. He had the old number but through all our ups and downs we both changed our number and never exchanged them.

I laid back and closed my eyes while periodically drinking the sweet poison straight from the bottle. An hour or so later and half a bottle left my phone chimed showing the unknown number again. I laughed and answered.

"Yeah."
"When you coming back this way?"
"I don't know why what's up?" I asked as if I didn't know what he wanted.
"Damn girl why you gotta make everything so difficult?" He questioned furiously.

I didn't respond just waited for the response I wanted.

"I want to see you Ziah, so can you bring yo ass back this way?" He asked sweetly with authority in his voice.

I smiled while staring up into the sky. I shut my eyes and silently gave God thanks.

"Yeah, I'm coming."
"Aright, drive safe please and just make it here."
"Ok." I hung up the phone and laid in the sand smiling because I was so in love with this thuggish, whorish, dope dealing, man from the hood, what a cliche.

As I got closer to the city I started to become overwhelmed about what was to come, *was he ready to give in or was he just trying to have sex.*

The thought of my energy finally colliding with his energy, feeling his warmth, allowing him to see my softer side flooded my thoughts rapidly. We both finally get to know one another from letting down our guards putting down our battle shields and standing in front of one another completely naked no armor or wall just us and our feelings. I wanted to show him how much I care for him, how much I wanted him, how I wanted to shower him with love. I had gotten so overwhelm about Fox that I failed to think through our possible encounter. I was making us more than it was. He could just want comfort for the night and I was his choice. My doubt about his feelings for me rushed in. I shook off the negative thoughts that crept into my mind. As I drove in my thoughts Tyrese Nothing on You played through the speakers. I smiled and was ready for whatever with this beautiful man.

I got closer to his street, my phone chimed and I answered it without looking at the screen thinking it was Fox.

"Heyy."

"Ziah where are you?!" Calais screamed through the phone.

I immediately recognized the panic in her voice.

"Cal what's wrong calm down." I replied into the phone.

"Ziah Fox has been shot." She spoke into the receiver.

My heart dropped and my eyes filled with tears that streamed down my face.

"What?! No, No I'm driving to his house to meet him now." I said through a raspy voice.

"No, Ziah he's been shot. I don't know how bad it is, but I just got a call.

He was at a gas station and some dudes tried to rob him. I don't know how many times he's been shot or what hospital he's been rushed to." She explained through a voice full of sorrow and tears.

"O' God no, don't do this please Lord not this again, please nooo."

"Ziah where are you? Where you at?" Calais asked again and again.

I pulled over and wept on the phone too heartbroken to respond at the time.

"Ziahhhh! Ziahhh, calm down and tell me where you at?" Calais screamed worriedly in the phone.

I couldn't respond at the time. My muscles went weak and my hand dropped my phone. He would die without me loving him. No one knows about our love. I wouldn't even attend the funeral to see all the women mourn and cry over a man they never even knew. I refuse to be among the conquest.

Lord, our Father God, I'm coming to you right now asking you to please spare him. Lord, spare Travis's life Lord and I promise I'll make it my mission to separate from him. Please don't take him from me Lord, not him. Spare him and I leave him alone. I'm not sure how or when but I'll depart from him. I'll walk away from him and his lifestyle if that's what you seek, but don't take him. I'll take my hands off of him, if that is your will, but spare him. I'll walk away if that is to be.

I sat in the parking lot of a closed down restaurant a few blocks from Fox's house weeping in my car not knowing what to do. Headlights pulled up in front of me, it was Calais she had found me. She told me to slide over and she jumped in the driver's seat. She waived whoever it was that drove with her off. She leaned over and grabbed me closing me in her arms trying to console me. She drove me to her house because I didn't want to be seen at the hospital knowing that all his chicks may be there. We said nothing just went straight to the back to her Jacuzzi and got in. She brought along some Peach Exclusive Vodka and an already rolled blunt. She turned on some music and we chilled in silence until we were so high and drunk we both needed to crash.

Months passed, Valentine's Day is fast approaching, Fox had made it out the hospital with no real damage but I hadn't seen him. I called him while he was in the hospital, spoke to him to be sure he was well. He went back to doing what he had been doing all along and at this point I was extremely hurt and done. I could care less that he started sleeping around again, it was time for me to focus on my daughter and get back to my goals. I started job searching and researching schools because I was ready to get out of Passion City and begin my life. Calais had started hanging out at her cousins on a regular and I knew there was a reason behind it. I know her. I started to do my thing as she did hers.

We tended to do this because we act so much alike but have different interest we gave one another breathing room. I had to find something better in life than what the average in Passion city is willing to offer.

Everyone seems so content with their small town lives they live in and I guess that's great giving they are thankful for what they do have…if it's that. I want more in life. I want my life to truly have purpose. I want to do great things and that won't get accomplished staying in Passion City seeing the same thing time and time again. I don't understand how Fox can have a near death experience and come out still taking his life for granted. I backed away completely to find out that he had gone and met up with all his tramps once he left the hospital. Honestly it hurt, I was hurt and felt the best thing for me to do was to lay low. He wants what he has even if it's not showing his true potential. I know Fox, he doesn't want the life he has he is just afraid of failure. He doesn't try to be in a real monogamous relationship because he doesn't want to fail at it so he does what is expected of him. He doesn't want to venture out the streets because he doesn't want to be rejected by life. Somewhere down the line he has implanted in his head that he isn't good for anything but the streets. The thought of this hurt because he is oppressing his true beauty, his talent, his capabilities and he is the only thing holding him back. We all go through struggles in life make bad decisions and have to find other ways around life but that makes the success that much better.

I shut my eyes to realize that Fox had been smothered. He could no longer see himself reaching his dreams. I sat in the computer room searching dental schools and it led to medical degrees. I had become intrigued about obtaining a doctorate in cardiovascular surgery. I begin smiling because I had found a new path. The same original goal just a different route that would lead to more opportunities. I also know that I had to gain a useful skill that I could be put to work, immediately, so that I can obtain employment. This I would keep to myself until I put it into work because I wanted no one else outside opinions influencing me or secretly wishing me to fail. I got off the computer and went out back to get some air. I thought about the plans I made for life and how none of them followed through except for my daughter. I refused to be discouraged because I know that God's plans for me is greater. I've always felt different since I was a child, there was something in life that never allowed me to feel ordinary but like my life has a great purpose and to obtain it I just have to let go and let God.

Much time passed and I had also found my own place and a self-employed job managing the purchase of exported and imported goods. I make my own hours therefore it works around my school schedule as well as I can work from home. I was accepted into graduate school a step closer to obtaining my medical degree. I found a three bedroom home in the woods with 2 acres. My daughter loved the home and the dog we both agreed upon getting. It is a small light brown Terrier my daughter name Benzie. I had gotten my life started up after taking a year off from school and a few months away from Calais, Fox and going out. I still think about Fox a lot and because I got another car I sometimes drove past his house to make sure he was still alive. I and Calais touched base with one another just to stay on the up and up. Avniel's dad constantly tried to make it work with us especially once I showed him I didn't need him for support but to cut that short I filed for child support to finalize our split.

One late Saturday in April, the sun was setting with a nice breeze in the air so I decided to sit out in a lawn chair with a glass of Pinot Grigio and a joint. I lay back in the lawn chair with my soft R&B playing enjoying my alone time since Avniel went with her dad for the weekends. I really didn't like having to share my daughter but I won't keep him from being in her life either.

I wonder what Fox was doing and who was the new thing in his life? Was she good for him? Was he being safe, careful, smart? I never wanted anything to do with the thug life, but I wanted everything to do with Fox. He just didn't want anything to do with me. I'm not the girl that he felt he was good enough for or could ever please. I thought of him often, it was a constant thing. He invaded my thoughts like a tumor and I wondered how I could remove it. No matter what I did he was always on my mind. I prayed for him and his safety every night. I prayed for his life, for his heart, for his intellectual mind to wise up and go for something more.

The sun was completely down, my torches were lit, I was on my third glass of wine and about to light my second joint when my cell phone ring. I looked down at the number but it was an unknown number.

"Hello." I answered chipper from the wine and marijuana combination.

"What's up?" The familiar voice greeted.

My heart dropped hearing Fox's voice on my phone.

'Hey." I greeted again not knowing what to say.

"How you been?" He asked.

"I've been good. You?" I replied still surprised to hear his voice.

"What you doin? You busy?"

"Uhm...no I'm just relaxing in my yard. Why?"

"Is that music in the background?" Fox questioned.

"Yes it is." I replied with a smile at his inquiring thoughts.

"You have company over? I mean I don't want to interrupt you…" He begin to rant on.

"No, no just me I'm relaxing calm down." I quickly replied through laughter.

"Nah, I just wasn't trying to interrupt anything. You could've been in the middle of something. I don't know because you don't fuck with me anymore."

I smiled knowing he had a lot on his chest to get off. "Nope, just me drinking wine and getting stoned in my yard." I laughed after revealing my scene.

He joined in laughter with me and told me I was crazy. I smiled knowing he says that in substitute of funny.

"Where ya' daughter?" Fox continued to inquire.

I smiled again knowing where his questions were leading to.

"She is with her dad for the weekend." I answered through my smile.

There was silence for a few seconds so I skipped all the small talk.

"You want to come keep me company?"

"Yeah, I can do that, give me a minute I'll be there."

THE BEAUTY -N- A THUG

"Hey don't you need directions?" I asked him having the feeling he already knew where I stayed.

"Yeah, where you at?" He went along with me.

"I'm off of Blanton, my house is beige just before you get to the gas station. It's blocked by a few trees, but the street is called Chester"

"Alright."

"Okay."

I hung up the phone and couldn't stop smiling. I lit up my blunt, smoked it, listen to my music in the silent night. I finished my first bottle of Pinot Grigio, went inside to discard the bottle and pop another. As I popped the top off the bottle, my doorbell rang and my heart skipped a beat. I sat the bottle on the counter and went to open the door. I opened the door to be met by Fox, his beautiful grilled out smile and a twenty four pack of Bud Light.

"Hey." I greeted as I let him into my home.

"What's up." He replied as he went to the kitchen and placed the bud light in the refrigerator. Once he finished he walked up to me as I was pouring my wine.

"Can I get a hug?"

I smiled, sat my glass down and embraced him. He smelled wonderful and felt even better. We embraced each other for a few seconds and then I led him outside.

"This nice Ziah, you like the woods huh? I laughed and nodded my head.

"I just like my peace, I like being away from civilization. I love the country."

He popped open his beer and sat back in his chair. I turned the music up and we sat there in one another's company, zoned and in peace. I could feel his energy because I'm high and spiraling in space. We had picked up exactly where we left off as if we had been hanging out this entire time. Our silence was broken.

"Why'd you disappear on me Ziah." I sighed knowing this was coming soon.

"I don't disappear Fox, I have a life I have to get to."

"So what you be just fuckin' with us to pass time, get off then back to your world."

"No, just have to get back to my priorities."

"Okay, I see you have priorities, but it's been months since I've seen you."

I didn't respond because I am under the influence of two substances and I know how this would end. I would get emotional and he'd run, so I would rather not to prevent him from taking my heart this time.

"Oh you have nothing to say." He replied sitting up in his chair with his beer in his hand.

I said nothing just look toward him. He was radiant even through his anger. I know this man, he didn't know how to deal with his emotions so it automatically transformed into rage. I sat up because there was no need to hold onto feelings I have for him, and then get upset when he didn't know.

"Fox last time I spoke to you, you were in the hospital and I was worried SICK about you. I was truly scared not knowing what condition you were in, I was scared of losing the only man I have ever…" I stopped myself from saying the rest.

"Nah, say what you were going to say, don't stop." Fox encouraged but I didn't continue.

"I've never heard you use that word, scared. Ziah, what does me being in the hospital have to do with anything?"

I gave out a smug arrogant chuckle to his ignorance. I stared into his eyes as he stared back at me.

"Absolutely nothing Fox." I replied sarcastically.

"See that's your fucking problem, I'm not a damn mind reader Ziah, if you don't tell me how you feeling, how am I going to know what to do with you?!" Fox yelled at me.

"By going off what you feel idiot. Why does it matter how I feel that determines what you do? You have your own damn feelings asshole go off of them?"

"You the fucking female get in touch with your feelings!" He replied. I laughed at his remark.

"I am in touch with my feelings, but being in touch and wearing them on your sleeve to be abused are two different things."

"Well how will I know how you are feeling Ziah? We been doing this for two years now. You are a grown ass woman act like it."

I stood up.

"I'm not doing this with you because you're an idiot."

I went to the kitchen and poured myself more wine. He stayed outside in the chair. I couldn't watch him walk out the door again because of our communication barriers. I also have an unwillingness to submit to his needs of blatant affection. I went to the bathroom and sat on the edge of the tub. I sat on the tub and drank my wine. I wasn't going to do this again. I'm so very much in love with Fox, but I am afraid to admit that to him because of the life he lives. I'm afraid he won't feel the same or pretend he does only to hurt me in the end. I'm afraid of him feeling the same and us not working out. I'm afraid he doesn't want to put in work with me because I am stubborn. I'm afraid he doesn't want to be a family man or he can't quit bed hopping. My fear was causing my mind to hide my emotions and I wanted to reveal them to him. I wanted to be with him and show him just how much I care for him. How much love I held for him, how much passion. I wanted him to trust and believe in me. I wanted him. Or are these all excuses to unveil my true fear. My fear of because of all the games, heartache, hurt, arguing women I couldn't really commit to him. I lacked trust in him because of being able to see him for him as well as the things he did. I said so many things about wanting to be with him and when he tries, I am the one who backs away because we have gone through so much I have developed a barrier that he built with the lies, deceit, and friendship. The friendship allowed me close enough to get to know him ,but also to see the the ways everyone spoke of. I've never known a love like this outside of my family for a man. Now here I am with so much passion for the biggest slut, the biggest dope boy in town and my inhibitor is the conflict within myself.

I finished my wine, reached up top of the mirror and pulled down another joint. I smoke the joint then exited out of hiding to air it out. I hit the corner to enter into the kitchen and Fox was standing at the back door with his back to the sliding glass with a beer staring at the moon.

I smiled and walked toward him, he turned around to greet me.

"I thought you had left." I could see in his eyes he was feeling his bud lights because he was more relaxed and in his zone.

"Nah, I'm still here, unless you want me to leave."

"No, I want you here."

"Ziah I don't really know what you've done to me but I haven't been the same since I met you." He blurted while facing me. I smiled at his honesty.

"I am so happy we decided to get to know one another and not just go off what people said about us. You are such a caring, sweet and kind individual, when you want to be." We laughed in unison. "Now that I have you in my life, I never want to lose you." I replied as I moved closer to him.

I caressed his thick eyebrows with my index finger, ran my finger down his nose, lips and chin.

"That was sweet of you to say." He commented.

"I mean it." I replied while caressing his cheek.

He moved in closer so that I was between him and the glass door.

"I've dealt with a lot of women Ziah, but you are different. You make me feel like no one has ever been able to. You are much sweeter than I ever imagined. You carry a lot of love inside."

"Only for you Fox. In order to get to you I had to let my guard down which I never do, but in the process I found something in you I'm not willing to let go."

He stared into my eyes as if he was examining my soul for the truth to my words.

"No lies here Fox only my heart."

As I said it, he placed his forehead on mine and his chest on my chest. I could feel his heart racing as he felt mine do the same. The moment was quite intense as we had made a small step. I had revealed to this man how much I truly adore him and the depth that it goes.

"Ziah how long have you felt this way?" He asked while still pressed against me.

I leaned up, kissed his nose and replied.

"Since I was fourteen, the very first moment I ever laid eyes on you."

He placed his hands on my sides and gripped them tightly. Our breathing became deeper as our hearts raced.

"You?" I questioned while caressing the back of his neck.

He picked his head up and I looked him his eyes to find soft vulnerability.

"The first time you ever shot me a bird."

I smiled and kissed his lips softly with such passion and force. *I did this all the time as a teenager everytime I saw him. I had heard of his reputation and was angry with a man I didn't even know and he didn't know me. I would see him around town and every time, no matter where, with no hesitation, I threw up my middle finger at him.*

He held me on the wall by my waist as we made love to each other with our kisses. I gripped the back of his neck tugging him into me. I wanted him. I needed to feel him inside of me. We had gone years with a curious love for one another and two long years with back and forth emotions that neither of us knew how to express.

We parted for air. I took him by the hand led him inside, closed the sliding glass door and led him into my bedroom.

The music was playing from Pandora, Kem's station and all the right music was streaming through the speakers. Fox stood in front of me waiting for me to make the first move to be sure we were really doing this. I ran my hand under his shirt and caressed his stomach, chest, and arms. I removed his shirt over his head and leaned in for more kissing. He removed my shirt and backed me to the bed. I laid down on the bed and he came down on top of me. He slid me out of my sweats to reveal my uncovered body placed in front of him. He kissed my stomach; his lips moved up my stomach to my breast as he caressed my nipples with his tongue and placed himself in between my legs. I reached beneath him and unbuckled his belt then his pants and slid his jeans down with my feet. His penis stood hard inside his briefs waiting to be revealed. I uncovered it, caressed it and with every stroke he lightly moaned on my breast until he could no longer take it. He kissed me fiercely while removing his pants completely.

While he removed his pants I grabbed a condom from the top drawer of my night stand. He placed it on, and then he laid on top of me completely naked, skin to skin and his touch changed. He handled me like I was fragile. He placed his right arm underneath my head and used his left to insert himself inside of me. The condoms were ribbed for your pleasure, the next best thing to skin. His thickness filled my walls and then some which caused me to gasp in pleasure, as he whispered with pleasure. He moved on top of me with force but in a sensual manner. We kissed while he gave me pleasure with each stroke, our bodies were in sync and moving in unison. He rolled on top as I did the same on the bottom.

We both made noises we couldn't contain from such erotic pleasure filled passion with each movement, each kiss, each stroke. We had desired one another for almost two years and we are finally adding the last piece of our connection.

"Go harder." I whispered.

He did just that and we both groaned louder with ecstasy and as we were both tightening up he grabbed my hand and locked it with his tightly. I rolled him so that I was now on top of him. I wasted no time, I immediately begin grinding my hips into his pelvis back and forth round in circles not wanting to lose our rhythm. He held my hips down as he thrust himself into me. I cringed with pleasure. I gripped his chest and continued to move not letting up so he tilted his head to the ceiling and shut his eyes. His body felt like it was stiffening up so he pulled me off of him to keep himself from climaxing. He got behind me and I lowered my upper body to the bed with my waist in the air. He inserted himself into my overwhelmed juice box and begin thrusting his pelvis into me. As he did I pushed my hips back into his pelvis making the contact that much more forceful.

Fox and I moaned uncontrollably like wolves howling at the moon. I gripped the sheets and he gripped my waist. I turned around to watch his pelvis thrust into my body and then I glanced up at him, just as I did he climaxed holding on to me tighter for support. We both collapsed onto the bed both breathing rampantly and fully satisfied. We both lie still wrapped in one another, my thoughts begin rolling in.

I found the strength, stood and walked into the bathroom to shower. I really just wanted to clear my thoughts, not knowing where this would leave us because I had finally given him the one thing I felt he desired the most from me. I got lost in thought as the hot steamed water ran down my body rinsing away the filth I had just created with the man I am totally and completely in love with.

His intelligence was astounding. His true personality was beautiful. His company is enjoyable; undeniably attractive; sex amazing and our connection was like no other. This is how I felt. I have no idea how he is feeling. Fox has no stability, no monogamous bone in his body at least that's how I feel. I may be what interest him now but who's to say how long that'll last. I want to spend my life with him. I want him to have him. I still couldn't tell him that, but why? I couldn't truly give him my all because I knew he would never appreciate it. He still didn't know how to be himself. So how can he really love someone when he didn't love himself. All his arrogance, conceited talk, gloating, tough guy attitude, it is all an image to hide his insecurities. He has finally given me his truth, but that's behind closed doors. This would be our little secret.

I was interrupted by a knock on the glass door of the shower. Fox stood in front of me with just his pants on revealing his hairy chest and path to his well-structured manhood. We stood staring at each other before I opened the door. I looked into his eyes as he did the same. I know exactly how I feel about the man in front of me. I know what would keep me from having him…Me.

I opened the door and he dropped his pants to the floor. I stepped back to the opposite side to allow him in. I had no time to react to his presence. He stepped forward toward me. He held my face in his hands and landed a kiss so familiar I leaned on the wall for support. It was the passionate filled kiss we shared in the Key West. He poured his heart into me through our kiss. I gripped his lower back to hold on to what we were sharing. His hand then slid down to my neck, as it did I dug my nails into his back. I squirmed with excitement from his hand being around my neck, his body pressed against me as well as his manhood piercing me. We pulled away to breathe. He slid his hands down to my hands and locked them. He leaned his forehead on mine with his eyes shut. I watched him show me a new side, a compassionate side, his vulnerability.

"Ziah don't hurt me, I'll do what I have to keep you, but don't hurt me."

I stepped off the wall for support and stability. I unloosened our hands to grip his neck. Our eyes met.

"Fox, the love I carry for you won't allow me to hurt you. I am so in love with you it scares me.

"What you scared of?"

I looked away for a moment then back into his deep brown eyes.

"Losing you." I replied with emotional depth.

He continued looking into my eyes before he kissed me. I wrapped my arms around his neck overlapping one another as I stood on the tip of my toes.

He squeezed each side of my lower abdomen. I dug my nails into his neck which aroused him even more.

PART II

UNVEILED EMOTIONS

 This girl had come out of the sky. She's from Passion City, I could say I practically watched her grow up and now she had me as open as the Grand Canyon. I knew there was something different about her. She's beautiful, her smile was so bright and unexpected that it was branded in my head the first time I saw it from across the room. She has the perfect skin color kissed by the sun, her hair a dark sandy brown, voluptuous breast, thick thighs and the smartest girl I've encountered. She was always so mean; she held her head upward with only the sky in view. I hadn't planned on running into her once she had become a woman and I got word she graduated from college. However there she was, right in front of me and without hesitation I invited her into my world.

 I really just wanted to fuck her. I watched her sway her hips countless times, enticing me and I had to see if she moved that well in the sheets. Before I made a move, I watched her laugh away nights with her best friend, no regards to anyone but each other. She drank as much as me and the boys and she always seemed so into herself. We started hanging and I saw her up close and she held my interest. She had me discussing everything possible with her except what I had sought after, sex. I would be in the house watching TV and she would send me a random text. After the text she was the only thing branded in my head. I had the boys come over while she was around to test her personality, but nothing changed; she stayed the same mean, giggly, rude chilled girl. She came off as a spoiled, stuck up college girl, but was actually down to earth, funny, tranquil and fun to be around when she knew you. We had formed a bond with each other and I begin to zone in on her as we all hung out. She smiled, she flirted, she chilled and she was spoiled. She and her friend had us catering to them with no effort at all and many times they brought their own personal drinks because they preferred a different taste each week. I had run through a lot of girls near and far, beauties, but none had the effect on me she caused. I tried to get a grip but found myself picking arguments with her, intentionally getting her involved to see how she felt about me. She indulged and we locked in on one another often, with an audience, but I couldn't figure this one out. She showed interest but nothing noticeable by others. I knew because I had gotten to know her on a personal level, alone time. When we were out on the same scene she ignored me. She zoned in with her best friend as she always did and they laughed the night away. She had come for me like a torpedo and I had no warning, didn't know what to do.

 I begin cheating on my girl, bouncing from chick to chick, bed to bed, trying to rid myself of her invading my thoughts. Through it all, I wanted every encounter, every girl to only be her, including the one I was dating. I didn't know what to do with the things I was feeling, the way I wanted this girl. I craved her, but nothing ever happened. She started to disappear every once in a while and I knew she had been involved with someone and they had a baby. I clenched my fist countless nights while I was alone to think of him touching her, entering her.

 The Key West trip me and Darkness took with her and her friend opened a door that became too heavy to close. We had gotten involved but in an emotional way.

 She had me kissing her like she was my woman, my love, my wife, but she wouldn't go any further because I had a girlfriend she would say. I chuckled at the thought of that trip many times, to think of the emotion she had me showing that I felt would never exist in me. I've been playing the game since I was a git, running the streets, getting money, running with my crew and smashing girls. I had girlfriends, many of them, but they meant nothing just chicks

I cuffed to show they were tamable. I've slept with friends, siblings, rivals, I've had them all and none lasted. I met them all, the ones claiming to be real, riders, virgins, bull daggers, professionals, wives, girlfriends, strippers, name them I've had them.

They all weren't what they said; none lasted because they didn't live up to my expectations or what I needed a woman to be, my only. I had thought I was in love a time or two but it turned out to be for the birds. I had given up on finding my one and was preparing to be a bachelor forever, and then she came along as cute as could be.

Our encounters when she was a youngster amuse me. She had animosity toward me, she disliked me in the worst way, I thought it to be cute. She never hesitated to insult me with a flick of her finger regardless of where we were. As a young girl she had so much spirit, personality and strong will. She played sports and was quite rough. Her personality did not fit her face, she looked as if she should have been in beauty pageants or primping in mirrors, but she was out in the yard playing tackle football, flipping with the boys and being viscous. Several times I saw her I laughed, she was not your average girl in Passion City and once she had become an educated woman, she became more refined but with that same attitude. I hadn't realized how much of my thoughts she was taking up until every time I saw her coming, I couldn't stop my heart from fluttering or my face from smiling. She made me evaluate myself and how I was living, I wanted more for myself, I wanted something better, I needed her. I didn't know how to get her so I begin drinking heavily, out of control and doing things I thought I'd never do, like step to her about not coming around as much.

Now here we were two years after hanging out and about thirteen years later from catching my attention, her standing in front of me telling me she didn't want to lose me. Ziah's eyes stared into me with truth, honesty, passion and love.

Her lips full, filled with color, her skin smooth and vibrant, her scent intoxicating my nose, her heart longing for mine. I wanted to give her all of me but didn't know how. I wouldn't allow myself to trust such a beautiful face. My mind wouldn't let me regardless of what my heart was saying. Why now? Why now did she confess herself to me what had changed? After so long she finally tells me she's been in love with me the whole time. She wanted marriage and monogamy, she wanted honesty, she wanted me and I wasn't sure if I could be what she deserved, what she needed. We have such different backgrounds I didn't want to ruin her or her future. I'm a street dude about money through my hustle which I mastered. I line my women up like my meals for the week, I have others depending on me to eat, and how would we work? She is a schoolgirl reaching for the universe, she had goals and dreams that she sought to accomplish with diligence. I run the streets with force, power and strategies. My life is unsafe and not suited for a woman like her, but I'm not willing to give her up, loose her to the next.

I opened my eyes to be greeted by Ziah sleeping with such serenity and peace. The sun radiated her skin through the window. We had been chilling together for about a good month and a half. I went to shower before she woke up.

I heard the sink running to see Ziah brushing her teeth. Once she was done she got in the shower with me and begin kissing my shoulders and caressing my back. My manhood instantly reacted to her touch. She slid her hands around me and moved them down to my stiff appendage. As she caressed me, I tilted my head back on her until I could no longer stand the sensation. I turned around and pinned her against the wall while tasting her tooth paste. I lifted her on the wall to rid us both of our morning desire.

She caressed the back of my head,

"Well morning handsome." She greeted me as I inserted myself into her warmth.

I smiled as she let out a moan from the feel of me.

"Mornin'". I replied.

She felt so snug, I wanted to stay inside her all day and night. The love I have for this woman along with the great sex was messing with my head. I know she has class today as well as her daughter was coming home and even though we are together now, I missed her. I hadn't felt like this about a female in such a long time, but I would never show her or anyone else how much I was in love with her.

I sat outside at the trap house with the usual gang, questioning me about my whereabouts these past weekends. I said nothing just gave a grin not wanting to reveal who I was with. They all grasped for straws about who I spent the weekend with. Their guessing game gave me a bad vibe because they name so many women as a possibility I started to wonder if I was the right man for Ziah. I didn't like where my thoughts were headed so I stood to retrieve a beer from the house.

"Ya'll boys fools man."

"You not gone tell us?" Slim questioned. I shook my head and entered the house.

I got a beer out of the fridge and sat in the living room a while to control my thoughts. I thought about Ziah and Slim, and I wondered if she knew I knew about them. Then I drifted to my boy Max, Slim's little brother, which led to Kay, one of my boys that went to college. I laughed to know this chick had been with my family yet she had me contemplating spending my life with her. She had been with them at different times in her life and none lasted past the first encounter. I laughed even harder to know how vicious she was in the bedroom. I knew why they didn't last, girl got game and moves. I like the fact she had book and street smarts. You don't find that in many girls from Passion City. I sat in the couch sunk down trying to get my thoughts together because it wasn't a good thing to be working with clouded thoughts. I ran numbers in my head to get my mind right.

There was a soft knock at the door that interrupted me.

"Yeah!" I called.

"It's me, Nat." She responded.

I exhaled not ready to go through the works with these females. I stood gathered myself and opened the door.

"What's up?" I asked with distance between us.

"The usual." She replied while moving closer.

I knew how this would go so I stopped it before it started. "I'm out."

"Are you serious?" She exclaimed.

I nodded yes as I opened the door for us to exit out. She was with her mom who hung with my mom so I kept my respect. Natalie was a regular customer but she came for more than the drugs. She happened to catch me one day drunk and offered me a jab and me being me I took it and couldn't get rid of her. Then again there was many of my female clients that happened with.

I sent her and her mom on their way and walked over to the fellas.

"Well we know it wasn't her." Darkness blurted with laughter.

I held my head down laughing. Then I leaned back knowing this day was going to be a good one.

Throughout the day just about every girl I've smashed within the past few months stopped by to 're-up' and they all wanted me to make them feel special in some way as if we have a special connection.

"Damn boy, what's going on? Whoever she is she got ya nose wide open."

Old Man Smith stated. I grinned as a picture of Ziah in the shower flashed in my mind.

All the boys started laughing and making jokes at my expense, I just sat back and chilled.

The sun begin setting, we turned up the music and vibe amongst one another. As I thought the worst was over and couldn't wait to see my girl that red Oldsmobile pulled up. Everyone simmered down and watched my reaction.

"There's the one." Darkness commented.

I gave him a look and walked toward my steps not wanting to deal with this one.

"Fox I know you see me!" She yelled.

"And?" I replied while locking my door.

"What you mean and?" She screamed while walking toward me.

"What's up man, what you want?" I asked her.

"What I want? Why you not returning any of my calls?" She question loudly causing a scene.

"Let's go in the house." I demanded not wanting her to cause a scene.

We stood in the kitchen going back and forth about me not answering my phone.

"I don't go with you girl." I replied.

"So that don't mean you have to disrespect me." She proclaimed.

"Disrespect you, how am I disrespecting you if I don't want to talk to you?"

I questioned puzzled. I laughed at her insolence.

"Ain't shit funny, so you don't want to talk to me now? Why? What done changed?"

"I just told you I don't want to talk to you, now get in your car and get down the road." I stated while walking toward the door.

She followed behind me.

"Don't walk away from me while I'm talking to you, don't be rude." She yelled while snatching my arm back.

"Gone girl, is you retarded or something?"

Just as I thought it couldn't get any worse, I opened the door to see a black nissan coupe had pulled up. I sighed knowing Ziah and her attitude.

All the boys started inquiring who was in the car because she hadn't got out yet. Natalie didn't care she continued patronizing me.

"Fox, you hear me talking to you." She yelled while coming down the steps.

I was focused on Ziah and hoping she was in a good mood.

I heard her door open and started walking toward her with Natalie yelling my name.

"FOX! FOX! I know you hear me. How you gone just walk off while I'm talking to you? I don't give a fuck about who in that car." She yelled while walking behind me.

Ziah stood up and walked from the driver side door, which stopped Natalie in her tracks. She walked up to me and we embraced one another in front of everyone. Ziah walked passed Natalie toward the yard, with me grinning behind her.

"Hey fellas." Ziah spoke to everyone not acknowledging Natalie.

"Fox." Natalie called my name once more. I turned to look at her.

"Come here." She beckoned me. I shook my head and kept walking.

She still trailed behind me.

"Travis." She called my name I stopped turned and laughed at her.

"For real though? This what you doing?"

"Fox, come open the door." Ziah called out still ignoring Natalie.

I walked toward the door with Natalie in tow still talking. I walked up the stairs looking at Ziah, hearing silence in the yard as she watched Natalie, daring her with her eyes to come up the steps. I opened the door and let Ziah walk in first not even turning around just shutting the door behind me.

I prepared to deal with Ziah, but she said nothing. She wrapped her hands around my neck and kissed me. She lifted my shirt over my head and continued kissing me. I kissed her, gripped her back then lifted her shirt over her head. She unbuckled my belt as I led her to my bedroom. I smiled as I watched her eyes quickly observe the room for any evidence of foolery. I wanted her even more and knew she was the woman for me. I laid her on the bed and showered her body with kisses. She tugged my jeans down as I tasted her nipples.

I leaned up to observe her. "You miss me?" I asked while she pulled her pants off.

She stopped to meet my eyes and smiled at my question.

She kissed my lips as she took me in her hand and slowly rubbed up and down my shaft. The softness of her touch sent chills all throughout my body.

"You know I did." She finally replied with a smirk.

"I know." I stated with confidence.

Months have flown by, Ziah and I hadn't spoken since the day she popped up over. We didn't exchange text as she usually did and the one time I called her she didn't answer the phone. I thought about her. What she was doing but it went no further because I felt if she cared like she say she did it would not have been that easy to walk away and without any notice, just cut off. I felt I was let off the hook because I'm not ready for the things she is.

Friday night had come in early September and I called Ziah's phone and got no answer once again. I said I don't want the things she did but here I am pursuing, chasing her, missing her. It had been two months since we chilled together or even spoken. She was out of class and her daughter should be with her dad by now. I kept getting no answer. I waited a while to give her time to hit me back but she hadn't. I had gotten agitated and felt like I was kissing her ass, like I've become too attached so I got dressed to step out for a while, clear my thoughts. I got to the scene parked and posted up with the boys. I was throwing drinks back like it was nothing. People came and went, music played and females flocked but I couldn't get my mind off of Ziah. I wondered if she had someone knew and didn't let me know.

"Hey I'm out of here." I announce to the boys.

"You out, already?" Old Man Smith asked.

"Yeah."

"Alright."

I got in my car and drove which led me to Ziah's house. Only her car was in the driveway and even though my pride told me to keep driving, my heart had me park. I sat in the car watching her house to see if she had left with someone else, maybe she was out with Calais. Then I noticed her car was running and a light from inside was on. I stepped out of my car and walked up to hers. She texted my phone telling me to get in the car. I went to the passenger side and slid in. She had 90's R&B playing and she looked high. She looked at me and smile. I didn't know what to think at this point.

"Long time no see, how the hell are ya'?" She asked laid back and mellow.

"What you mean I called you twice? You didn't pick up or call me back. So I said fuck it." I replied to her.

She begun laughing and threw her hands over her face.

"I wanted to see if you would fight for me, but what a bust that was." She admitted.

"Ziah what kind of shit is that. Don't be testing me and shit. Training me or whatever the hell it is you doing." I informed her.

I don't know if I was relieved, pissed or amused by her actions.

"I apologize Fox." She commented while turning her body toward me.

She isn't the type to apologize so freely, she has a lot of pride when it comes to her emotions so I knew it was the weed.

"Ziah, be straight up with me, tell me what you want."

"No, I want you to give me what it is you think I want."

I sighed at her statement, because it never could be a-b-c with her she always had to throw numbers, symbols and all in the lineup.

We sat in the car talking until she played her CD. *Anthony Hamilton Her Heart* came on and she turned it up. She zoned into the song and I watched her.

She moved her hips in her seat, she shut her eyes, she snapped her fingers and song. I watched this girl vibe out in front of me and I wanted her. She lit another joint and before I had a chance to let my window down she locked the door and the windows from her side. She knows I don't smoke, not the type to do my own product, it leads to bad business. She leaned her seat back and propped her feet in her seat. The thick smoke slowly climbed all over the car. She burned the joint in no time. I watched this intelligent beauty reveal herself to me beyond her appearance every time we encountered. What she called her flaws are the things that intensify her beauty.

I reached over and stroked her hair and her eyes followed my hand back over to me. She stared into my eyes with intensity. She was high and I find that unattractive for women to smoke but her eyes lured me into her. She rubbed up my arm, to my neck, to my eye brows, where she softly stroked them. She then perched in her seat and came in my area to place her vibrant body in my lap. I immediately grew hard. She placed soft kisses on my lips, my neck, my forehead, my cheeks and my ears. She used both her hands to caress my arms up on both sides. They met at the back of my neck in my hair. Her touch raised all the hairs on my body. I pulled her mouth into mine. Her kisses felt like a form of sex and it sent a rush of intense excitement into my body. She reached down and leaned the seat back. She adjusts herself to straddle across me. I didn't resist her but was surprised at the fact she wanted to have sex in the car when her house is a few feet away. She leaned into my ear and song part of the song to me. I realized this song was about me so I tuned in as she sat in my lap singing softly. She sent chills down my spine. This girl had me spent and I was falling in deeper with each encounter. She is nothing that I had imagined but so much more. She went back into her seat, but to undress herself. I watched and grew hungry for her as she slowly removed every piece of clothing from her body. She took her hair down and let it fall to her shoulders. Once she was completely naked she begun undressing me. Every moment I was more and more interested in the girl in front of me. She took our clothes and put them in the back seat. She stroked my body causing a stiff erection. I pulled her into my seat and she straddled across me allowing our bare bodies to touch. I indulged in her warmth with my fingers causing little moans to exert from her. I caressed her sensitivity with my fingers causing her body to stiffen with pleasure. She held onto my shoulders with her head tilted back, eyes closed and her mouth slightly open, no words or sounds escaping. I continued to embrace her warmth, took my other hand and brought her neck to my mouth to taste her body. She could no longer take anymore so she placed herself slowly down onto me. The pace she set was slow in rhythm but deep and hard in stroke. My hands held her waist and her hands gripped my hair while she rode me with frequent kisses. The music played soft and sensual notes with meaningful words that I felt neither of us knew how to say but the music said it all. Her body started to tremble and soft sighs came with each stroke. Her sound turned me on while she rode me so I gripped her harder, while thrusting into her. I needed to have all of her, I wanted to mark her insides, plant my flag because she was mine and I had to keep her. We moved in unison as she climaxed one after another out of her control, she had become so wet I was groaning from the pleasure of her insides. My body jerked and stiffened so she rose off of me quickly leaving me in both of our sex.

 She sat in her seat halfway redressing to go inside, so I did the same. We walked to her door and went inside. I went into the bathroom and turned on the shower. As the steam grew in the bathroom I ran my entire head under the water because I was experiencing an unfamiliar ache in my chest. I placed my hands on the wall in front of me and leaned forward lost in my thoughts.

 Damn, Ziah had me tripping. I felt my heart pounding uncontrollably as if it could be seen beating. There is a tight pressure in my chest and my stomach is in knots. I inhaled deep and released it to loosen my chest. *My thoughts are filled of Ziah, her smile, her laughter, her walk, her thoughts, her touch, her ambition her beauty her love her character. I am shook by the girl, everything she does draws me in closer to her. I keep trying to fight this feeling but it's pull, force, the passion is too much to let go. I could feel her heart when we were just having sex and it beat to the same rhythm as mine. Damn, she had opened her heart to me but who would have known the power and force it carried. Her heart was like the gravitational pull of a black hole and once you've entered, there is nothing in your body strong enough to pull away.*

I ran my hand down the front of my face to the statement that was just branded in my mind. I washed and exited the shower pondering whether I should stay or leave because now I had crossed over into forever leaving whatever happens, happens in the shadows. I sat on the couch not really watching TV just there zoned. I replayed the moment we had just had in the car that was filled with so much passion and eroticism that neither of us spoke then or now. Ziah came bouncing out of the room chipper in a tank and some small spandex shorts. She bounced right into the kitchen and several minutes later sat down next to me with a tray of snacks. I begin laughing at her knowing she had the munchies.

"You mighty happy what'd you find some more weed in the bathroom?" I questioned comically.

She turned and smiled at me not saying anything just smiling. Our eyes locked in on each other for a few moments until we realized we had gotten lost in one another. I stood to retrieve a bud light from the fridge to shake myself of this love spell shit. When I sat back down Ziah had turned down the lights with only the two lamps on either side of the couch lit. She was scrunched up on the couch eating, zoned to the max.

"You really shouldn't be eating all that shit." I comment while tossing my beer back.

"And you shouldn't be drinking." She quirkily replied.

I laughed, "What all you got over there?"

"What you want?" She asked.

"Naw, I'm good I don't eat after nine." I informed her.

She burst in a hard laughter. She continued to laugh for a while leaning over on me.

I chuckled at her contagious laughter. "You crazy girl." I proclaimed while drinking my beer.

She leaned back up straight and tried to refrain from laughing but slight giggles slid out.

I watched her as she lit up the dimly lit room with her smile. She enticed me every second we spend together. We sat and watched *In too Deep* as she ate her snacks and I was on my third beer. Through the middle of the movie her knees dropped from being scrunched into her chest symbolizing she was comfortable and open. Spending so much time together allowed me to pick up on Ziah's body language and expressions. We have gotten intimate numerous times now but a part of her still remained guarded which always showed in the beginning whenever we got around one another.

See I came from the streets and I did what was needed to survive. I did better than a lot and accomplished a lot in such a short bit of time. I understand that there is more than being 'hard' to make the money I do. There is a certain character you must possess to draw others to you. You must create a desire for the consumer toward you and be assured your product is the best. I had to also know how to strategize, run numbers and stay ahead of the game. My mentality was that of a businessman from college but I was the only one in my group that hadn't gone to college. I have encountered many different types of people, observed them, watch them, their movement and now I am really good at reading others.

As I thought to myself, I begin to feel as though I had been sold by Ziah.

She carried herself with a certain pride to her from the moment I met her, no matter her situation she remained the same. She did as she pleased but not as she saw. In all she did she still was able to remain conservative and shy in the eyes of many and I was one of them. She lured you with her attitude, her body language, her style. Than introduced you to her product, her skills, her capabilities, as if she was applying for a job. Only thing is she decided what job she was willing to work, to put effort into. I have gotten to know her and we have similar ways. At times it seemed as if she went to school and became a more knowledgeable and refined thug. When she wants something she goes hard for it, draws it in, then sits back and waits for that thing to realize she had it. Her look is the secret weapon and her mind is the abductor

I turned to observe this beauty sitting next to me. She could feel me staring so she looked at me back.

"What?" She asked shyly with a smirk.

"What's with the smirk?" I asked, as if she knew what I had been thinking and discovered.

"You gone sit there in your head the whole night or you going to keep me company?"

She was so beautiful in a conservative good girl way. This was why I am surprised every time she does some freaky shit. There is nothing good about her but no one could say anything otherwise. She looked innocent and sweet and was neither.

She reached over and rubbed my eyebrows. I closed my eyes because it was something about her touch that was comforting. I could feel her love with every touch that sent electric vibes to my manhood. She knew my habits, my movements, my expressions. She held the heart of a thug. I licked my lips and glared into her face. She lifted her eyes to meet mine. I leaned toward her and she opened her legs to welcome me in. I kissed her nose then her lips. I rubbed up and down her thighs as we made love in our kiss. She grabbed the bottom of my shirt and pulled me over on top of her while leaning back into the couch. My hand slid up her body to her round breast, they were soft and full. My mouth became jealous of my hands so I moved my mouth to her breast. She inhaled and her chest slightly rose with excitement. She squirmed with anticipation.

She lifted my head, "No games, I want you now." She proclaimed to me with such desire that I wasted no time. I yanked her shorts down, and entered her. She let out a faint pleasured moan. I watched her face as I pleased her, becoming turned on by her expressions.

"Go harder." She whispered lightly.

I thrust my pelvis forcefully into her body trying not to hurt her at the same time.

"Harder." She whispered again.

I hesitated not wanting to hurt her.

"Harder, I can take it. Don't hold back, I want all of you."

As the words left her mouth I lost control and all sound turned into her and I again howling in ecstasy to the moon.

Ziah had become distant. She no longer wanted to get up with me as much anymore it had become her hitting me up every other week for a late night sex-a-thon. I didn't complain, I could still do as I pleased as well as feed my soul's desire to be with her and all of her weird ways that attracted me to her.

One Saturday in early November out with the boys, we all decided to have a cookout in the yard so I hit Ziah up to invite her she didn't answer so I left it alone. Old Man Smith and I rode to the store to pick some items up. As we walked toward the entrance I saw Ziah leaving out and I smiled until I saw a white dude throw his arm around her. She smiled at Old Man Smith and they embraced one another. She spoke to me as I kept a straight face not wanting her to know how I wanted to slap the shit out of her.

"This is Braden, Braden this is Old Man Smith and Fox." She introduced.

"What's up." The white boy spoke.

She said her byes and they continued walking to the parking lot.

"Daaamn… Daaamn." Old Man Smith repeated with laughter while going into the store.

I said nothing just brushed it all off not giving a fuck what she did. We aren't an item, nor did we talk about being together. She is just another one of my friends. We just fucking and that was fine with me, she gets that I'm not ready for all that other shit, I'm getting this money.

The day drowned out pretty slow and the crowd came with the night. The cookout had turned into a party and I was just about lit when I saw Ziah and Calais approaching. My stomach turned and out of nowhere I became angry. I stared into Ziah as she walked up and I could see all over her face she was trying not to smile. I guess she don't know who the fuck I am. She'll never get the satisfaction of playing me. I swigged my beer as her and Calais spoke to everyone altogether. They went next to Old Man Smith and posted up passing a joint around.

Initially that's how Ziah and I had ended up around each other for the most part, because even though she really isn't the friendly type she fucks with Old Man Smith hard. There has been times she kept her distance but she never fell back off him just chilled whenever things between her and I became too much.

They stood in a group with two other people talking laughing and smoking so I retrieved another beer walked out into the party and posted up with Darkness. I didn't think she would show up for some reason but she did and I'm drunk so I'm trying to keep my thoughts together and compose myself. I turned back to see what they were doing and she looked at me. I held so much anger for her and I didn't like that, I didn't want her to be getting to me. Hell chicks come a dime a dozen to my liking, I don't need to fuck her. Just as I zoned in my head, Maxine, with the red oldsmobile, walked up to me and Darkness. She hugged on me and I let her because I'm single.

I realized she always showed up when I'm drinking because when I'm sober I can never remember why I fuck with her. Maxine always told me how much she cares for me, how she wanted to be with me but she isn't the type you wife. She's good to have around because when I wanted her she was always on board never putting up a fight. She had no standards no goals, no dreams or aspirations she was working toward, just another girl that like the ride and didn't know when to get off. She showed persistence and I must admit I like that about her so I dealt with her. She has no loyalty because she was fucking me while I was going with her best friend but she is consistent.

I turned around once more but Ziah and Calais weren't there anymore.

I realized that no woman can be trusted except for my mother because the world has made people falter for anything.

THE BEAUTY -N- A THUG

I jumped back into the money hard, running more numbers than ever before. I had no distractions, I had females that I called to get me off but there was no staying over just business. My business had expanded and I no longer had to get my hands dirty I was building an empire.

Ever since we had entered into a new year, I've had an uneasy feeling about a few of my workers. There was no evidence or reason for the feeling just something in my gut that made me question this person's loyalty. I probably need to relax take some time off, step back because hustling so much had my paranoia up. I have so much money coming in from all over that I feel I'm surrounded by snakes. Instead of pointing anyone out, I'm just gone chill because whoever it is will slip up and be exposed. In the meantime I need to tighten up on keeping watch on all these little ass gits running round pretending to be gangstas. It definitely isn't like back in the day when we were younger. If you were down with ya' niggas there was no turning or betrayal. You tell ya' dude to hold ya' weight that nigga held it for you, can't trust that shit today. These niggas will flip on ya' for pussy let alone work and cash. I get headaches sometimes trying to hold down every aspect of this shit, the clients, the product, the connect, the constituents, the feds, the bitches that I keep around, so many people could hold my fate in their hands, if the wrong situation or confrontation happened. I have to know who to fuck with, who to do business with and then who they do business with. Through it all I stay searching for an alternative that could generate the same amount of money in the same time, a way out. My mind stay in motion, even in my sleep. I've lost so many to this game, seen so many fall and betray one another for a quick come up, so I trust no one. I often sit in the dark and think about Ziah, what she doing? Who she with? Is she happy? Does she think about me? I've wanted to call her but my pride stops me, picturing her with that white boy makes me say fuck it.

PART III

ZIAH

The morning slowly beamed in through my window and slightly sheer curtains to rest on my face. No class today, no work, my daughter is in school so I am left to my own demise. Once I got her on the bus I thought I'd be able to get some more rest. I've already studied for my surgical theory exam weeks in advance trying to keep my mind off of Fox. I've cleaned my house several times and now I am here on this morning with nothing to occupy myself. I pulled myself out of the bed, showered went to my lawn chair and lit a blunt. I exhaled slowly to enhance the high from each hit because if I am going to think about him I might as well do it the best way I know how.

Once I finished the blunt I set my phone to iheart-radio, plugged it into my docking station and it came throughout the house from every speaker. I sat down on my kitchen counter and zoned into my music. I didn't want to listen to my music because it made me emotional about all my experiences that never were what they could have been. What I disregard more than rejection is regret. The music made my heartache, my thoughts scramble and my soul cried.

I knew it was a hard chance to settle down with Fox. He isn't the type to settle with one female. I still wanted him. I realized that he had an inner being that cried out to only one person and that was the woman meant for him. He has such a kind heart and once all the layers have been peeled back he's a man worth knowing and loving. I think I just had some hope that the passion and love from my heart that I held for him could change him for the better. That thought brought me back to my mom saying every woman wanted to be that special woman to turn a thug into a man. I lost that battle, I heard he is in deeper than ever and that saddens me to know. I sometimes woke up out my sleep in the wee hours panting praying that Fox was okay. I always think about what could of happen if I had been more open with him in the beginning, but immediately dismissed the thought because he would have left me down and out full of hurt, sorrow and more regret. Then again, I am left that way still. The pain I felt the day I pulled up to Fox's and saw him and a chick coming out of his house, it took everything in me not to reign down hell upon them both. I let go of all the anger that was brewing in me and experienced our pure untainted love before I let go of my dreams, wants, desires and longing of an inevitable love with Fox. I made love to Fox for one last time before I faded away from him.

I love him dearly, so much I can't bare it sometimes. The love I carry for this man is more than my body is use to, it's new. I am willing to hurt and suffer because I can't be with him in that world.

Just thinking on the love made my body quiver with desire. I had to do something, let my hair down and have some fun or I'd become too consumed with emotions. I had to find an outlet to escape from my own thoughts…not sure if that's normal.

I drove around a bit before I decided to go to my uncle's to relax. I know my uncle Patterson is up with the school buses, so I went to talk to him. As I pulled up to the house he was sitting in his chair near his fire pit. I Got out my car and walked to grab a chair near him and he took a shot of Tequila. I smiled because even though it's early morning he was up and on it already. I had my time in that same way and it made me think of the days. A time when we had friendship, laughter and fun. I missed that.

"Hey Unc." I spoke as I settle in my seat.

"What you doing up this early?" He questioned me with a low eye.

"Nothing, just needed the woods for a bit." I replied while leaning back in my seat.

"Yeah, I'm sure. What's going on?" He asked me while taking another hit out if his Tequila bottle.

I sighed not wanting to talk just needing the peace of the woods and the morning air. I just looked away as he continued to ramble on as he always did when no one else wanted to talk.

As he talked and I looked out into the woods, my aunt Gladys came out with a joint.

"Hey Ziah, What's going on?" She greeted as she placed the joint in her mouth and lit it. I smiled at her because I had made it over right on time dealing with two early birds.

"Nothing aunty just relaxing." I replied with ease as to not get questioned too much.

My aunt and uncle love to question me until I gave them something, if I came off as suspicious.

"You want to hit this?" She asked referring to the joint.

"Hold up, let me hit the mufucka first." My uncle whined.

I laughed and we sat around the fire pit at 9 in the morning getting baked. I sat in silence just staring into the fire.

I decided to text Fox and if he didn't answer life does go on.

Me: Heyy

A few minutes passed before he replied.

Fox: Who is this

I laughed at his remark. This is what he use to do when we first started hanging out.

Me: sexual chocolate

I was waiting on another text but my phone chimed. I looked to see it was Fox and laughed knowing the name had amused him.

"Hello." I answered.

"What's up man?" He replied.

"Nothing much what's good with you?"

"Shit really just getting to the money, you know."

"I hear ya." I stated hearing in his voice he had detached himself from all emotion.

"Damn, sexual chocolate, where you come up with that shit from?" He asked me through partial laughter.

"Coming to America, I knew you'd like that." I admitted.

"So what you been up to man?"

"Same, school and my daughter." I informed realizing I hadn't been out in a while.

"That's what's up."

"What you doing? You home?" I asked him.

"Yeah, watching the football highlights." He responded.

"Can I come over?" I asked.

"Over here? Now?" He replied inquisitively.

"Yeah, unless you have company or expecting company."

"Naw, I'm not expecting anyone, come on." He answered nonchalantly.

"Ok, I'll be there in a sec."

We hung up and I rested at the pit for a little while longer before I got up to go to Fox's house.

I had on some baggy yellow puma sweats a tank and some white sandals.

My hair is in a messy ponytail but yet I looked as though I had spent hours getting ready when in all honesty it took a few minutes. I arrived to Fox's house and text him to open the door. I got out of my car and he held the door open for me. We hugged one another as I entered into the house. He smelt delicious as always and dressed to impress even while chilling in his house. I laughed at my thoughts and realized I'm high. I took a seat on the couch and he sat down next to me with his back in the corner.

"So what's up man, you look good. What's been up with ya'?" He interrogated me while sizing me up and down with his eyes.

"Just been chilling keeping to myself with my head in the books." I replied while adjusting myself. I pulled my legs into my chest and leaned back.

"It's been a minute; I mean what made you want to come over?" Fox continued with the questions.

"Just wanted to check on you see how you doing?" I responded while staring at him.

"How the white boy doing?" Fox quizzed.

Before I answered I just looked at Fox knowing where he was going to take the conversation. He was ready to let me have it, argue, bicker and cause problems.

"Most likely at work, but I'm not too sure."

Fox smirked and turned back into the TV.

"Oh he has a job, where he work?" Fox asked as he flipped through the channels.

"Really, I'm not going to have this conversation with you." I proclaimed.

"What, I might get tired of making all this money and need to find something for less. But what's up though, what you need?" His demeanor changed.

"Nothing much I wanted to see how you doing?" I informed him.

"Oh I'm good, real good can't complain." He replied quickly while watching the TV.

"Are you?" I implemented with a deeper meaning.

Fox paused and looked at me then burst with laughter.

"Look Ziah don't start that shit man, I don't have time for it."

"I'm not but I know you Fox. The stuff you have doesn't compensate for how you doing."

"You know what you might be right, but I don't have to worry about that stuff betraying me or being bullshit. I know what it's here for which allows me to know what I'm dealing with." Fox responded coldly and distant as a hit.

The words were sharp like a blade and I immediately felt the pain. He stared me down with such hate and agony in his eyes and I sat speechless at his attitude toward me.

"So what does that mean? If you have something to say, say it." I had grown tired of his tough guy act toward me.

"I have nothing to say Ziah and if I did I would have said it. Nothing important or worth mentioning, feel me."

Every sentence had become stab after stab and I could feel he was holding back so I helped him.

I gave a soft giggle. "You know that's always a problem you had, never knowing how to accept the way you feel, brushing things off which is why you find yourself surrounded by inanimate objects and people with no substance."

"You know what fuck you Ziah, I don't have time to listen to your bullshit."

Fox stated.

"You know, you have so much potential to be amazing but you'll never be anything more than a dope dealing, bed hoping womanizer because you're afraid to do the unfamiliar, afraid to try, afraid of failure; with success Travis comes failure because you're pushing down barriers."

"Naw, I'm stacking money can you say the same? As a matter of fact get out."

He had grown irritated with me and I now had him where I need him to be.

"Travis, you are so dumb. Why must you sell yourself short, when you have all this yet you are still unhappy. And betrayal, you wouldn't know the first thing about loyalty giving you have not one person in your life you trust. You can't even be with one person because loyalty is not in you. You're full of hate and mischief because that's all you've known." I spat at him not making a move to leave.

"How the fuck you gone talk about loyalty. Get the fuck out Ziah, get out of my house." He demanded as he stood.

"You fucking idiot, from the first kiss all I wanted to do was give you all of me but your dumb ass is so caught up on an image and being that dude that you disregarded my feelings to be someone you can't even stand. You thought I'd play the fool for you, that I'd be sap for you. NO, I love you with every flaw of yours, ready to show you that all you need is one but you were too caught up on failure and being that guy that you couldn't even open your heart to me even though I could feel your love. So yea asshole I can talk about loyalty because that's all I wanted for us but you were too blind to see me apart from all the others." I lashed out as I stood to meet him.

"How the fuck when you skipping around town with a fuckin' cracka' and fucking me."

I laughed at his comment knowing this is what he's been holding back.

"Yeah, and you around here still flossing with every chick in the city while you caught up with me. You don't think I can see how you feel. I'm not one of these chicks Fox, I'm not after anything you have, and all I wanted was your mind. You gave that to me and guess what I can see you now, your feelings, your thoughts, you. So fuck all that shit you talking. I see you." I replied.

Once I said what I needed to I walked toward the door but I could see I had gotten to him. He reached out and pulled me back so that my back was in his chest. We stood that way for a few minutes and our hearts beat to the same rhythm. We both took the time to calm down because we've hurt each other with our words before and it led to us not talking for months. I closed my eyes as his smell navigated into my nose. I relaxed on his chest and laid my head back. He wrapped his arms around me and held on. I caressed his hands and arms. My hands traveled further up behind me to stroke his dreads. He slowly rubbed my hips as he placed his lips on my neck. I shut my eyes knowing where this was to lead, wanting this feeling I held for him to disappear because he would never be who I needed him to be.

"Let me go Fox." I requested as we both said nothing.

"You let me go." He responded referring to the grip I had on him but with an underlying meaning such as mine.

"I need to." I stated with meaning.

"Well why don't you?"

I unraveled us to turn around to meet his deep brown eyes full of knowledge, hurt and curiosity.

I kissed him with force bringing him down to the couch behind him. He gripped me and placed me on top of him. I took his shirt over his head and unzipped his pants. He rolled us and pulled my sweats completely off. He pulled my shirt up and tenderly caressed my nipples with his tongue. I rolled him and we landed on his brown fluffy carpet. I spit on his fully saluted manhood and drove down on top of him. He let out a groan I had never heard. I released my love over and over on top of him. I rode him with long hard strokes of vengeance. Those strokes transitioned into soft sensual love and passion. I had to relieve myself of these deeply engraved feelings for Fox because he would never want what I wanted for him, for us.

As soon as we were done I wasted no time getting dressed. I fixed myself as he was just getting off the carpet. I made sure I had all my things and headed to the door to leave. I stopped turned toward him and smiled.

"I want to let you go Travis, but you're the only man I've ever been in love with so it may take longer than I'd like. You were out of my control; my heart's running that show." I left and shut my phone off.

FOX

March had come full of cloudy days and long nights. So much had happen in such a short amount of time and I slowed my money flow down due to one of my houses being watched by the feds. I had brought in enough money to sit comfortable invest in a few things to keep me flowing but hustling had not only been about the money but something to do to keep my mind from thinking too much. I often found myself sitting around getting wasted to escape the thoughts that haunted me. Ziah and I hadn't spoken since that last morning she was over here and I hadn't heard anything about her because she was no longer hanging out. My pride stopped me from going to see her, not knowing if she had gotten back with her baby daddy. Her words burdened me each and every day since the day we had it out. She had come and disrupted my life once more and I despised her for it. Even though she was right, I still was fine with just being alive. The fact that I could have possibly given up a life I have always longed for, to maintain a status that I hated and placed a death wish on me, filled me with anger and regret. This beautiful intelligent woman with a future as bright as the stars wanted to commit to me give me her all, but I pushed her away afraid of not being able to give her what she wanted and needed. This fucked with me every day I awoke, no matter what those thoughts crept in at some point. I found myself dissatisfied with the women that surrounded me always asking for a handout and having nothing to talk about but gossip. This was just another day in March that's cloudy.

Even though I had slowed my business down Darkness kept his running in full throttle. He had put a new guy on that had just been released from the state.

His name was Zany and he like to pop pills that caused him to dance all night.

Darkness had brought him in but he stayed around me trying to get in with me. I dealt with him but that was Darkness's runner and I made sure to keep my distance as well as an eye on him.

Early Monday morning in the beginning of June, I sat back and propped up on my couch trying to watch TV, but realized I had run out of beer so I took a trip to the store. I know it's too early to be out buying beer but I'd rather do it now before the roads became busy. Pulling up to the store I parked as Ziah was walking out. I hopped out my car and saw that she was surprised to be running into me at such an early hour after avoiding me.

"Hey." She greeted.

"What's up with you?" I greeted back trying to keep my cool but I was happy to see her.

"Same old thing." She replied while shifting uncomfortably.

"So why haven't I heard from you?" I asked her with bluntness.

She smiled. "I'm trying to let you go."

I laughed at her comment. "Oh yeah…how's that working for you?"

"It's a process because I think about you every day, I miss you like crazy and I worry about you." she responded with honesty.

I smiled and moved in closer to give her a hug. We pressed our bodies together and I felt her love pouring through the hug. It was nurturing and enclosed. I felt my body grow weak, I didn't want to let her go, she had gotten to me. I needed her but I don't know how to tell her that and she wouldn't believe me. I wanted to take her home and never let her leave but I had to make some changes in my life first.

"It's nice seeing you Fox. Be safe and smart." She reminded me as she always did.

I smiled knowing that she really meant those words. She has always meant them I just was too caught up in the streets to truly hear them.

"You too Ziah."

We both stood there wanting to say so much more but no words would come and neither of us would start so we departed from each other slowly and went our separate ways.

When I pulled back into the yard I noticed Old Man Smith was here. I laughed because older people didn't fake when it came to starting their day. He was standing by the fire smoking a cigarette. I was happy to see him because I need to relax and he was the only man I would trust to be truthful with me.

"I'm right on time." He commented as he saw me pull the twenty four pack of beer out of the car.

"What's sup old man?" I greeted while he opened the cooler for me.

"Same old thing." He responded. That made me think of Ziah and how she had just said the exact same words.

"What you doing out this early?" I asked.

"Tell you the truth I got up this morning and felt like being here. So here I am."

I smiled and took a seat on the table as did he.

"What's up boi?" Old Man Smith questioned me.

"Nothing man. I just seen Ziah." I revealed.

"Oh yea, how she doing? I haven't seen her in a while."

"She good, being Ziah." I replied with soft laughter.

"What happen?" Old Man Smith asked as he popped the top of his beer.

"I think it's about that time I slow down man. I need to find something else to put my time into, it's time for a change." I stated to myself but audible for Old Man Smith to hear.

"Whoa…that's something I haven't heard you say in a while. But yea, yea, it's that time because things will get worse before they get better with your work. No one can be trusted anymore." Old Man Smith spoke his knowledge.

"Nah, no one can be. It's just getting more dangerous not being familiar with who you're surrounding yourself with."

"Now are you serious about this or are you just talking?"

I took a second to really search myself.

"Nah, I'm serious. I want more from life, not the type of things you can buy."

Old Man Smith lowered his beer from his mouth as he was preparing to take a sip.

"Boi...you in love?" Old Man Smith asked inquisitively.

I looked at him, "I don't know." I answered with all honesty.

"Who is it? Ziah?"

I held my head down trying to find the words to respond to his question but nothing would come so I said nothing.

"I'm not going to lie, she's hell, and sometime she make you want to choke slam her," he chuckled as he did the motion, "but I can see she truly loves you, has been for a while. She's alright, I like her, good head on her shoulders, but won't take no shit." He stated as he continued to chuckle. I laughed with him at the truth about her.

"You ready to tell her?" Old Man Smith questioned.

I shook my head because that was a question I hadn't asked myself. How would I tell her after all this time, all the fights, would she believe me. So much had happen with us and she still carried the same love for me, maybe even more than what she started with. Could I be what she needed? Give her what she expected? Be in her life completely? I'll never know unless I try.

ZIAH

Mid June brought rainy days but this beautiful Saturday Avniel's father and I decided to take her to a water park. We rode down the 50ft slides, splashed in the fountains and enjoyed ourselves. I could tell that Avniel had been waiting on the moment to be with both of her parents once again and I loved to see how joyful she was. I honestly did enjoy our outings together and it made me contemplate giving us another try. I'm not attracted to him anymore and have no feelings for him but gratitude, however if I can't have Travis then I wanted no one else. I gave my heart to Travis and I gave him all of it, so I had no more to give to anyone else, therefore I'll settle with the familiar and hope that the emotions come later.

We arrived back to my house late in the evening and because Avniel was already asleep I put her in her bed. Braden kissed her goodnight and we exited her room. I walked into the kitchen, poured myself a glass of Moscato and grabbed a beer for Braden. We went out back and sat in the lawn chairs.

"It's nice out here Ziah." Braden remarked while observing my surroundings.

"Thank you. I love it out here."

Braden stood and walked out into the yard. I observed him because of my thoughts of reconnecting with him. He is such a gorgeous guy, dirty blonde hair, deep blue eyes, and average height with a lean body. He loved wearing hats and both of his ears were pierced. He is of Jewish and German descent so his nose was pointy and sized. When I first met him I had to have him. He was my first true interracial relationship and I was his first black girl. We couldn't get enough of one another. We had sex everyday throughout the day. As we progressed he had habits that I didn't agree with, as did I, but I dealt with them. As the years passed I noticed we had a bit of a rage problem, things had gotten off balance and we had begun to become a hindrance to one another.

"I want to ask you something Ziah." Braden announced as he took a seat next to me.

"Ok." I replied as I sipped my wine.

"Look, I know things haven't been good between us for a long time. We both have gone our own ways to experience life. I don't see myself getting married to anyone; if I were it would be to you. You've been by my side for some of the roughest things in life and I'm grateful to you for that." He reached over grabbed my hand and knelt down on one knee.

I gasped and my heart raced.

"I love you so much and I feel you're my soulmate, we were meant to be…" He pulled out a white box, "Will you marry me?"

I stared down at the sparkling 3 carat princess cut diamond that was being presented to me and all I could do was think of Fox. I didn't know what to say and tried to get Fox's face out of my mind. I wanted to say yes to move forward with my life and stop waiting on Fox to change, stop hoping that he could become the man that I need him to be, but my mouth wouldn't move.

I stood up to catch my breath at a higher altitude.

"O' my. Are you serious? We haven't been together in so long." I replied.

He stood to meet me in height.

"I know Ziah, but I only love you, only want to be with you and don't want to loose you to the next to come. I need you in my life. I want to be a family."

Braden declared as he exposed his feelings to me.

"Yes…yes I will." I answered quickly before I could shut down.

He placed the ring on my finger and lifted me in the air. He kissed my lips, my hand, my cheeks and my arm.

"Thank you so much, I love you."

He went inside the house as I stared down at my finger and sat in my chair. He came back out with my bottle of wine and a blunt in his hand.

"It's time to celebrate. You have made me the happiest man in the world."

He said as he grabbed my hand and kissed it again.

I smiled at his gesture, tilted my glass back and poured another. He lit the blunt and we zoned out.

Could I marry him without being in love with him? Did I want to? Oh God I am at a lost for words right now. Is this in your plan for me are you directing me to let Fox go and move on with Braden because he's better fit for me? I had been instructed to leave him for You to place him back in my life. I couldn't help but wonder would there be consequences from me accepting this proposal. I can hear Braden next to me protesting a long engagement like the last time but to just go to the courthouse next week and have a big reception. This is the end of Fox in my life. I was being made to move forward and let him go. This was life telling me he isn't going to change so get on with your life. Right. The things Braden said about only wanting to be with me and being soul mates is how I feel about Fox. I wonder if he feels the way I feel about Braden, toward me. Am I just some girl that fell in too deep and he didn't want to hurt my feelings? I was never that important to him but because of how much he saw I felt for him he went along with it. Had I took my feelings and magnified them creating this desired love between the both of us when he had no clue of what he felt or needed? I had set myself up to think I was something special to him, when he has never known true love even if it bit him on the ass. Well here's to you Travis I pray you have longevity and prosperity in your life and finally find what it is you need.

    Tears formed in my eyes and fell down my cheeks as I raised my glass to the sky and sipped. Braden noticed the tears and wiped them thinking they were tears of joy. We laid out, burned and watched the stars until I sent Braden home.

    Monday morning as soon as class had let out and I got home I called Calais up.
    "Hello." Calais answered.
    "Hey, what you doing?" I asked wasting no time.
    "Shit. What you doing?"
    "I need you to come over…like right now…right now."
    She let out a giggle. "Well what's wrong?" She asked.
    "Just get over here." I declared.
    "Ok, I'm coming."
    Calais arrived twenty minutes later and as soon as she walked in I showed her the ring.
    "O' shit, you getting married. Fox?" She asked while observing the ring.
    "No Braden, he asked me Saturday night." I informed her as I lit a blunt and dropped to the couch.
    She let out laughter.
    "Braden, I thought you was done with him?"
    "I am, or I was…I don't know he just proposed and said I'm who he wants to marry so I said yes." I told her truthfully.
    "Well what about Fox?" She asked while sitting next to me on the couch with a beer.

"He doesn't want me." I stated bluntly.

"He said that." She asked in disbelief.

"No but he didn't have to I can't wait for him to grow into a man." I replied.

"Well it's not fair to Braden to marry him because you can't have who you want.

You not in love with him." Calais informed me.

"I know…I'm horrible but if I can't have Fox then I'm marrying Braden." I affirmed.

Calais said nothing else just drank her beer and I smoked my blunt.

"I don't know what to do Calais. I don't want to wait for Fox to make up his mind or even wait for him to notice me. But no I am not in love with Braden, I'm not even attracted to him."

Just as I said it Calais spit out her drink.

"What? Ziah that's not right, you can't marry him." She yelled through laughter.

"I don't know it can come later." I said with a smile and hope in my voice.

Calais laughed at me as I continued to smoke.

"How the hell when you're a sex addict?" She proclaimed with a smile.

"I am not!" I responded.

"The hell you not! Your sex drive is overactive shit." She screamed.

We both laughed out with amusement and hadn't realized we had gotten buzzed. Calais, like always had caught contact from my blunt, her drink and we had such a great vibe going.

"My mom's really excited, way more than I am." I told Calais.

"I bet she is, you know she hate Fox."

"She has Avniel so Braden and I can celebrate but he has to work all day."

I told Calais as I put my blunt out.

"Well get changed, we'll celebrate. You haven't been out in a while." She commanded me.

I went to my room to do just that.

"Hey guess who I seen coming from Darkness house." Calais yelled back from the living room.

"Who?" I screamed back to her.

"Maxine, with the red oldsmobile." Calais shouted back.

I walked back into the living room shirtless at her discovery.

"Are you serious, that's Fox's, let see what'd he called her… straggler." I revealed.

"I know girl, seems she been fucking Darkness too, but I don't think Fox know."

"Wow." Was all I could say as I walked back to the room to finish getting dressed.

FOX

I had just made plans to get out of the dope business and a kilo of my cocaine had gone missing. The money that generated from that kilo is all that I could think about. Around twenty five grand had just been snatched from my hands and no one knew where it went. Once again in this new day and age there is no loyalty and no trust amongst anyone. Everyone claim they didn't take it and even though we all work together there was not one person who didn't have suspicion about someone else in the business. I felt as though it's a damn shame a background check is needed to obtain a street job now a days. I had no hope of discovering who the deviant was. However, I would keep an eye out for my shit because it's distinct and pure. If the mu'fucka is smart he'll go at least two counties away to distribute because my name travels distance. I had to calculate the loss and try to compensate for it in marijuana. I decided to have a night out with Darkness and slim to get some order and dismiss a few dudes I suspected.

We decided to have our night out at Smith's Gentlemen's club. Slim came along for the party and once he saw naked ass flopping throughout the establishment he was no longer in his right mind. Darkness and I took a seat at the bar facing the stage. We ordered drinks and he lit up a Cuban cigar.

"Fuck I can't believe we got hit from the inside. I can kill a mu'fucka bout my money." Darkness vented through low eyes.

"Nah man, just a minor set back." I responded.

"Minor set back nigga they got us for a kilo, how the fuck?" He restated with more anger.

I leaned back and watched the first dancer up slide down the pole while sucking on a red lollipop. Darkness called over the waitress and we both got change for a grand.

"Man honestly, I been thinking about getting out this shit, going legit." I revealed to Darkness while we both watched the dancer.

"I think it's about that time these niggas can't be trusted out here. What'd you have in mind." Darkness asked while he tossed some money at the dancer as she did a split while in a handstand. She was pierced and neatly shaved so I tossed a few as well.

"I don't know yet." I replied.

I had been getting a weird vibe from Darkness like something was up with him. I don't like the feeling because he been my boy since we hit puberty but my heart was uneasy. Ziah had been right, I have no one in my life that I fully trusted other than Old Man Smith and that even had grown thin. I had doubts about him in the beginning but was immediately proven wrong after all the times he saved me from trouble. Darkness always had my back but did his own thing at the same time. He's never given me a reason to question his loyalty but I know him and something was up with him. I knew exactly how to do it. I had to verify his loyalty before I became business partners with him on a different scale.

I ordered a round of shots for us but let slim take mine and Darkness was in party mode so he didn't notice. All I had to do was get him drinking and eventually being around all this ass he would be ready to pop some ecstasy.

Once the ecstasy got in his system his mind would be on one thing and he'd tell me what I need to know. We ordered more drinks and tossed money on the chicks with the best moves or the best yang. I paid for Slim to get private treatment in the back which left me with Darkness. He was high on marijuana and ecstasy and laughing at all his own jokes. I was still working on my second drink.

"So what's up man? What's been going on wit ya?" I casually asked as he played in a dancer's yang.

"Bruh, you already know. Trying to get this money." He responded.

I nodded in agreement.

"That's what's up. Anything new going on?" I asked while tossing a few on the dancer in front of me.

"Nah, shit the city don't have shit to offer, ya' know." He replied while leaning back from the dancer.

I ordered another round of shots for him and I, this time I took mine. I asked him nothing more and waited for him to come to me. We watched the dancers, got lap dances and chilled. Just as my stomach was settling that he had nothing to tell me, just under the same pressure as me he told me.

He looked at me once…twice… "Bruh…" he called. My stomach tightens and I knew he had a secret to reveal.

"What's up?" I responded casually while taking a sip of my vodka and sprite.

All I could think was this nigga betta not tell me he took a kilo of my shit. This nigga betta not tell me he lost my money, this nigga betta not be with the fuck shit I expect from everyone else and not him.

"Bruh…I fucked Maxine." He blurted over the music.

I didn't know how to respond to that. He had been acting weird because he fucked some bitch. He thought I had ties to her so he felt he betrayed me. So even though he felt like I had feelings for her he still fucked her and that made him feel guilty.

"She came on to me one night I was wasted in a club took her ass to the car she sucked me up and I fucked her." He continued.

Even though she means nothing to me, I'm not going into business with someone who has no loyalty.

"Nah man you good. She a hoe and she's not mine…have at it." I consented.

I'm entering into a different level of business which one needs to be professional, have respect and boundaries. Even though Max doesn't mean shit to me, he thought she did yet he fucked her. That speaks volume and I'm listening loud and clear.

I got up with Old Man Smith in the next few days and checked out some property for me to open a dinner club. Passion City use to have much more value and substance back when I was a git coming up. Even the street runners had more respect about themselves. The hoes handled their business with pride and dignity. I wanted to bring back that feeling, that vibe that once was, not this shit that's going on now. Kids being brought up with no morals or values, no real teachings like I was taught back in the day. The dinner club would be called Beauty. It would have live Jazz bands on the weekends, a place to eat, drink and dance to music with meaning and substance. Young adult night on Thursdays and it would be built like a speakeasy. There will be a dress code and bouncers.

Passion City would come alive again and have something that wouldn't be an embarrassment to claim.

Old Man Smith and I found the location built to the right size just a few adjustments needed. I had finally felt content and like I was making a step in the right direction. I knew once Darkness found out he would question me and why I hadn't included him but this, this would be mine, my establishment, my project, my portrayal of Beauty. We drew up a business plan and begin arranging for hire.

We had to search for a food and liquor service to partner with as well as a décor.

In the middle of all the business Ziah came to my mind.

I had taken a step in the right direction with the pieces falling into place. I had finally made up my mind to leave the streets. I recall how instead of calling me a drug dealer Ziah would call me a businessman and told me my mind had no limits because of the potential she saw in me. She showed me even in the dark world full of lies deceit, betrayal and superficial people there was still hope for true beauty. She had grown up in the same city as I did, knew the same people, yet all of her innocence was protected. She had never been hurt, never been betrayed, never really felt the cruelty of the world other than death. She still had a pure heart untainted by manipulation. She still believed in romance and true love which she wanted with me. The bad guy that everyone labeled me as.

The guy everyone told her to stay away from. The guy her family told her she was wasting her time with. She wanted to share her heart with me, and she showed me that there is still beauty in such an ugly world.

The following Saturday morning I woke up feeling great as if God was smiling upon me. I showered and placed myself in front of the TV but didn't have anything to watch. I turned the TV off and sat in the silence. I hadn't talk to God in such a long time but it's long overdue. The last time I truly spoke with him was when I was laying in the hospital bed after I had gotten shot. Now, it's been placed on my heart to give him some of my time and speak with truth. I sat up and begin speaking.

My Heavenly father,

I know it's been quite some time since we've had a chance to talk. To be honest, I didn't think you wanted to hear from me because of the life I live. I asked you to spare my life so that I could have the chance to tell the woman I love how much she means to me, how she has touched me but then I didn't, I didn't think I stood a chance with her, that we could work, I didn't have enough faith. I've done so much in my life I felt like even if I called, you wouldn't listen because of all the sin I am drowned in. Lord, I am thankful to you for sparing my life allowing me to see these days even if they are disturbing at times. I know I'm not your favorite person to hear from but I truly thank you. I am ready to change Father maybe even go to church. God there's this woman that has changed my opinion on life and what the world has to offer, she's amazing and I'm in love with her.

That had been the first time I had said that out loud and it came as a shock.

I ask for your forgiveness my God for all of the bad shi…things I've done please forgive my soul and allow your son Jesus Christ to come into my life to show me the way I shall go. Thank you, Amen

ZIAH

My sister and Calais had taken care of all the reception arrangements. I just had to focus on my final exams and getting to the courthouse. Once I told Calais I was going to go through with the marriage, she would text me every morning asking if I was sure. I never responded each time she did but I did laugh at her persistence. I would be getting married in four days, July 12th. Each Day I awoke, the first thing I wanted to do was to call Fox. However, I didn't. I had to get him out of my system and focus on my future. This is how I thought but not how I feel. I woke up out of my sleep every night at four in the morning with anxiety thinking of Fox and wondering if he was ok. My heart hadn't gotten the memo to move forward, he didn't want the same things as we did.

Any time I had with nothing to do I spent it thinking of this man and how I wanted it to be him I was marrying. I threw myself in my school work, tending to my daughter and her school work. I participated in Avniel's after school ballet classes by serving refreshments. I volunteered to take my grandma out because she would occupy my thoughts with her over active mind.

Two days from my adventure to the courthouse I sat out in my lawn chair with my daughter in my lap. We listened to music and watched the stars. She lay on top of me and I had finally given up and exhaled. I still secretly hoped that Fox would find out and come rushing over to stop me. He would tell me he couldn't live without me, but a girl could dream.

Avniel asked me a thousand questions and I answered them. She truly worked every nerve in my body asking me questions about the universe but I could only smile at her curiosity. She thought that her mom was all knowing. She fell asleep on top me so I put her to bed. As I walked back to the couch my phone chimed.

"Hello." I answered.

"Has he called yet?" Calais questioned.

I gave a chuckle to know I wasn't the only one still holding out with hope.

"Nope." I replied with no emotion.

"He must not know Ziah. Are you really going to do this?" She asked with sadness.

"It doesn't matter if he knows. He doesn't care so I have to let him go. And why not with Braden the father of my child?" I blurted with a hint of anger.

"Yeah, you're right, but I mean if that's what you want to do."

"Yes Calais ,it is but thanks for being concerned."

We talked a bit more and hung up. I didn't want to waste any more time holding out for Fox or even thinking about him. I made the decision to move forward and that's what I'm doing.

FOX

Friday morning came with a slight breeze as fall was slowly arriving to claim her time. July had been a hot fiery son of a bitch, but today was nice. I sat out in the yard and saw Calais pulling up and I hoped she had Ziah with her. She hoped out of the car alone dressed up.

"What's up man? Where you headed?" I asked checking out her attire.

She walked up to me and took a second before she spoke. I felt my stomach tighten knowing she had no good news.

"Fox I just came by to tell you…Ziah's getting married today, in a few hours actually." She informed me.

My heart sank, for a minute I forgot Calais was standing in front of me. I took a second to regroup and respond.

"Well tell her I said congratulations." I replied silently trying to clear my thoughts.

"That's it Fox? Well she's getting married at one at the courthouse, just in case you were wondering." She reveal as she walked back to her car, got in and drove off.

I sat in that spot for an hour in my thoughts.

I had lost her. I let her slip away from me because of my pride and she was now going to belong to someone else. How could she just marry someone else if she loves me the way she says? I never did tell her how I feel about her, that she was the only true woman I had ever encountered. It's fine we had some good times and she deserved to be with someone that would make her happy. I just can't help but wonder why in the hell she would marry someone else if she said she only wanted to be with me. Fuck it! Fuck her! It's not the first time someone I truly care about has left me, won't be the last time. Damn Fox, get over yourself. She's settling because she can't have that with you. Are you ready to lose the only woman who has ever really known you? The way you think? To someone who will never understand her value? Fuck!

I dialed Ziah's number but it went straight to voicemail. I didn't know where she was or how I could get to her. *I had to catch her at the courthouse before she entered.* I dashed inside the house to freshen up and put on clothes. I grabbed my keys and locked down my house. Just as I reached my car four men in all black approached me. I sighed at the timing, I tilted my head to the sky and unlocked my door; shots were fired and I felt a burning sensation in my neck, side and legs. I dropped to the ground with nothing but the sky in view as I heard feet hit the pavement. I struggled to get to my feet but my blood was leaving my body too quickly so I was weak. As I lay on the ground I smiled to know that I would meet my maker seeing beauty. I didn't want to go to hell, because true beauty resided in heaven

Now I lay me down to sleep, I pray the Lord my soul to keep, if I shall die before I wake, I pray the Lord my soul to take, Father forgive me of my sins.

ZIAH

I stood in the hall in my white dress trying to calm my nerves with Calais and Taylor. Taylor went to find my mother and Calais fanned me.

"I went and saw Fox today." She confessed.

I stopped pacing and focused on her.

"What? Why?" I questioned with curiosity.

"I thought he should know." She answered.

"And..." I asked with curiosity.

She hesitated..."He said congratulations."

Tears came to my eyes and I had to sit down. Calais sat next to me and we waited for the wedding to begin.

I walked down the aisle toward Braden with a smile but hurt in my heart.

My entire family had piled into the courtroom to witness Braden and my union.

We spoke our vows and exchanged the rings.

I could not have been happier to get to the reception to get stoned out of my mind and drunk until I was unbearable. I arrived to my reception with Braden attached to my hand and we entered the room to a beautifully decorated building that was white and yellow. I had gotten married to not the love of my life but a man full of love that I would now try to reconnect with. I didn't see Calais yet so I went into the ladies room with a few of my cousins and aunt and we all got stoned. We passed three blunts around and a joint to celebrate my union.

I can do this. I can love this man. I can treat him as he desires and hopefully rid myself of Fox and move forward to be happy. My family is happy. My daughter is happy. I am super high.

I laughed out loud to my thoughts and everyone else laughed at me. We left out the bathroom high as hell and in good spirits. We could hear the music coming up the hall and we were all ready to party. I walked into the reception hall with my hands in the air already moving to the music to focus in on my mom and Taylor talking intensely in the corner. I paid no attention because they always had something to discuss. I then saw Calais who was teary eyed as if she had been crying.

"Calais what's wrong?" I asked noticing her mood.

She said nothing but I saw my mom and sister rushing over to us

"Ziah let's go out here for a second. Come on Calais." My mom directed as she led us out of the reception hall into an office. Calais cried hard as my sister and mom tried to talk to me.

"What is going on!" I screamed as I begin to panic.

"Ziah..." My mom begin but her voice cracked and she stop to hold back her tears.

"What the fuck is going on, where is Avniel?" I yelled with confusion and fear.

"Calm down Ziah." My sister told me as she took the lead. Calais still drowning in her own tears.

"What is going on?" I asked through rage.

"Ziah…Fox is dead." My sister announced.

The news hit me like knives stabbing me in my heart. I panted trying to catch my breath, unknowing tears flowed down my cheeks.

"What?" I asked with more confusion looking toward Calais as she had just told me she went to see him.

"He was gun down Ziah about…about an hour ago. He was found in his yard.

They rushed him to the hospital but it was too late he had lost too much blood." My mom spilled to me through sorrow.

I stood up wiped my tears and went out to my reception. As I entered the hall everyone had received the same news as I did and watched me walk toward my table. I hurt Lord knows I hurt so bad I felt as if my heart had been removed from my body. However, I would not allow this moment to become about everyone trying to console me over something they didn't understand nor did they approve of. We would celebrate and I would have my time later.

I drank everything that was placed in front of me. I had my first dance with my new husband, and I partied…all in vain.

This was my fault. I had given up on Fox. I lost hope and faith in him and my ability to get to him and accepted another man's hand in marriage. I had fulfilled my vow to God. Fox had been left alone to his own demise. How could I do this? How could I just walk away from the only man I have ever been in love with, not willing to fight for him? Now he was removed completely from my life and I had to be left with all my thoughts and pain. I couldn't change my mind because he was gone. I love him more than he'd ever know and he loved me more than he'd ever show.

It took me a few months to make it up to Fox's dinner club. The whole city had been raving about it but I hadn't been ready. I didn't attend the funeral, I couldn't. I left town with my daughter for a week to a cabin in Montana to calm my spirits. Braden and I still stayed in separate homes because I wasn't able to take anymore steps with him at the time. My heart was filled with sorrow, despair and hurt. I cried every day at the cabin while my daughter and I sat out at the lake looking out into the open woods. She tried to console me each day never asking what was wrong with me only hugging me and showering me with kisses.

Early one day in the middle of February of 2014, I pulled up to a red brick building, double hardwood doors that led into a palace decorated in a 1920's styles theme. I smiled at seeing the beauty of Fox's brain, which quickly brought tears. I walked around and observed every inch trying to get a feel of Fox's last accomplishment. As I stopped at a window and took in the view of a lake, I thought how beautifully placed the scene had been as if it was out of a picture. Old Man Smith walked up behind me.

"Hey girl." He greeted me.

I turned to embrace him holding him longer than I wanted to but not able to let go.

"I know, I know." He comforted me while patting my back.

I finally let go and tried to clear my face.

"So this is really nice." I complemented trying to lighten my mood.

"Yeah, all Fox's idea. His plan to get him out." Old Man Smith stated.

I turned to look into his face.

"To get out…like out of…" I didn't have to finish before Old Man Smith nodded in agreement.

He showed me around the place and all the memorials dedicated to him in various places before I left. There was one that caught my attention Fox had instructed to be placed above the VIP section. It read:

The love a woman carries for a man cannot save him. The love a man carries for her will change him.

I drove home in silence.

I got home, checked my mail and went inside. The words on the wall stuck in my head. I needed to something, so I lit my blunt and sat in my lawn chair in my thoughts.

Travis, why didn't you tell me you were getting out? How could you not tell me you were ready to change but let me think you had no courage? God, I love you so much even now. Know that I never stop loving you, always praying and hoping the best for you. I will truly say that I found my gentleman in a thug, that held the passion of a romantic, the pride of a noblemen and the heart of a warrior. I guess I'll see you next lifetime, because you have my heart still. I will never let your heart go, but one day I shall return it. You will forever be missed but never forgotten, I love you Fox.

I blew the smoke from the last hit of my blunt into the air and watched it carry my thoughts to the sky.

www.ingramcontent.com/pod-product-compliance
Lightning Source LLC
LaVergne TN
LVHW091933070526
838200LV00068B/971